SECRET AT
PEBBLE CREEK

Books by Lisa Jones Baker

The Hope Chest of Dreams Series

Rebecca's Bouquet
Annie's Recipe
Rachel's Dream
Secret at Pebble Creek

Anthologies

The Amish Christmas Kitchen
(with Kelly Long and Jennifer Beckstrand)
The Amish Christmas Candle
(with Kelly Long and Jennifer Beckstrand)

Published by Kensington Publishing Corporation

SECRET AT PEBBLE CREEK

Lisa Jones Baker

ZEBRA BOOKS
KENSINGTON PUBLISHING CORP.
http://www.kensingtonbooks.com

ZEBRA BOOKS are published by

Kensington Publishing Corp.
119 West 40th Street
New York, NY 10018

All Kensington titles, imprints, and distributed lines are available at special quantity discounts for bulk purchases for sales promotion, premiums, fund-raising, educational, or institutional use.

Special book excerpts or customized printings can also be created to fit specific needs. For details, write or phone the office of the Kensington Sales Manager: Attn.: Sales Department. Kensington Publishing Corp., 119 West 40th Street, New York, NY 10018. Phone: 1-800-221-2647.

Zebra and the Z logo Reg. U.S. Pat. & TM Off.
BOUQUET Reg. U.S. Pat. & TM Off.

First Printing: September 2018
ISBN-13: 978-1-4201-4744-5
ISBN-10: 1-4201-4744-7

eISBN-13: 978-1-4201-4745-2
eISBN-10: 1-4201-4745-5

10 9 8 7 6 5 4 3 2 1

Printed in the United States of America

Acknowledgments

I've often heard that it takes a village to raise a child; however, it also takes a village to write a book! First and foremost, I thank my Lord and Savior for all that I've been given. I'm fully aware that the gift of publication comes from Him.

Huge thanks to my parents, John and Marcia, for their constant love and support, and for raising me in a loving, Christian home. My patient librarian/reading specialist mother listened to me read my nearly thirty books out loud without complaint. Warm thanks to my beloved friend in heaven, Gary Kerr, who made time to trouble-shoot computer issues and story ideas at all times, day and night. His passing left a huge void in my life. To Beth and Doug Zehr, who do it all! Thank you to idea-filled Aunt Velda Baker, who has a keen ability to catch even the smallest detail. Talented Lisa Norato, true friend, confidante, and critique partner, has worked with me on numerous projects. Thanks to *New York Times* bestselling author Joan Wester Anderson, who helped to launch my writing career, and also to hundreds of writers who have helped me to hone my writing skills for nearly thirty years. Of course, I couldn't go without crediting my Amish friend, who prefers to remain anonymous, but who answers questions and reads my books from cover to cover to check that my stories are consistent with Amish life in Arthur, Illinois. I have so much respect for you.

And I couldn't forget the friendly folks in Arthur who have contributed in too many ways to list. To my friends and family, who were with me during my twenty-four-year journey to publication, and last but not least, huge thanks to agent-of-the-year Tamela Hancock Murray, brilliant editor Selena James, publicist extraordinaire Jane Nutter, and the great team at Kensington. *Secret at Pebble Creek* is for all of you!

Prologue

Years Earlier—During the Lifetime of Sam and Esther Beachy

Sam Beachy's heart warmed as he added finishing touches to the beautiful piece of oak in front of him. To his right, a hope-chest lid he'd started rested on a felt cloth. To his left, another piece for a young grandma-to-be waited for completion.

Inside of his old barn in the quiet countryside of Arthur, Illinois, the bright July sunlight poured in through the open windows, enabling him to better scrutinize the detailed lines of his newest project.

He held his special work in front of him. Sam gingerly exchanged his carving knife for another tool from the worn holder and continued to hone the fine details.

For years, he'd etched pictures into hope-chest lids, and by now, the skill came so naturally to him, he could create depth to make his art appear real by using his knife and other tools at different angles.

Only this particular project wasn't a hope chest. With a slow, steady motion, he ran a finger over the rounded, smooth edge. A squirrel quietly appeared next to Sam's sturdy black shoes and stood on its hind feet, extended its front paws, and held them in a begging position. As Sam stared into two round, hopeful eyes, he laughed and stopped what he was doing.

"You think I was born to feed you, don't you?"

As the brown mammal stayed very still, Sam got up from his chair, reached into the sack of treats that he kept next to him while he worked, plucked a lone pecan, and bent to give it to the small furry creature.

While two pigeons hovered at the top of the ladder leading up to the hayloft, the squirrel didn't hesitate to accept the morsel before scurrying across the barn to the open doors, where he finally disappeared. The moment the beggar was gone, a loud whinny filled the air.

A few yards away, Strawberry, Sam's horse, trotted into his stall, where he sucked up water from the deep metal trough. Afterwards, he threw back his head and clomped his hoof to an impatient beat.

Letting out a deep breath, Sam put down his work, got up, stepped to the animal's stall, and gently stroked the long nose of his pal. "Strawberry, I know you're lookin' for Esther's sponge cakes. But I don't have any."

He extended his fingers in front of him to show empty hands before dropping his arms to his sides. He touched the animal's nose with his pointer finger. "Be patient. Esther's making a fresh batch right now. *Jetzt sofort.*"

In response, the young standardbred nudged Sam's chin with his nose. Sam caressed the long, thick, reddish-brown mane with his fingers until the horse closed his eyes.

Sam regarded the loving creature that had been named

by his dear wife, Esther. The mere thought of Esther made his heart melt.

As he thought of the petite white-haired woman he'd known his entire life, emotional, joy-filled tears filled his eyes, and he blinked at the salty sting. "Pal, God blessed me with Esther, and do you know that next year we'll celebrate sixty years of marriage? *Sechzig.*"

The only response was a shake of Strawberry's head to get rid of some flies.

"I've made her something very special." He lifted his chin a notch. The buzzing of flies was the only sound. "It's going to be hard to keep the secret for nearly a year."

He furrowed his brows while the horse brushed against Sam's forearm where his shirt sleeve was rolled up. "I know this might come as a surprise, but this time, it's not a hope chest. But . . ." Sam let out a satisfied sigh. "It's the most special gift I've ever made."

The mouthwatering scent of Esther's desserts floated from the open kitchen windows all the way to the barn. Sam's stomach growled. But right now, there wasn't time to think about food. Even if they were sponge cakes baked by the best cook around.

Whenever Sam focused on a project—and right now it was his hand-carved gift for Esther—his mind was one-track. He lived and breathed each special story that he captured on wood.

And right now, this present required serious thought. Where to keep it. What clues to write to help Esther find it.

And the hiding place wouldn't be just anywhere. *Nein.* It would be at their special spot. Where Esther had agreed to spend the rest of her life with him. The place they called "their own."

Sam dropped his arm to his side and shoved his fingers into his deep pants pockets. When Strawberry nudged him, Sam lifted his right hand and continued caressing the spoiled standardbred.

But as Sam stroked the long nose, his thoughts weren't on the needy animal. Or the squirrels that counted on him for treats. Or his Irish setter, who kept Esther company while she baked. Or his next hope chest order.

"Esther." A combination of great affection and emotion edged his voice as he said her name. A loud snort temporarily pulled him from his reverie, and Sam moved his fingers to behind Strawberry's ears. The horse lowered his gaze to the cement floor and held very still.

Feeling the need to talk about his secret plan, Sam began thinking out loud. "Strawberry, I'm going to tell you something that no one else is privy to."

Sam moved the toe of his left shoe up and down to a quick, excited beat. He could hear the long branches of the tall oaks brush the top of the building. In the background, chickens clucked. Through the open doors, he glimpsed horses in the distant field. He knew the man behind them being pulled on a small platform.

As Sam acknowledged his nearly six decades with Esther, he shook his head in gratefulness and squeezed his eyes closed to pray. "Dear Lord, I give You all the praise and thanks for my marriage, for our four sons who are with You, and even for our needy four-legged family members."

He paused to clear the uncomfortable knot from his throat before lowering his voice to a tone that was barely more than a whisper. "Thank You for helping me to make my most beautiful carving for Esther. And *denki* for our special anniversary that we'll celebrate next year. Amen."

Fully aware of the beautiful day on the other side of the walls, he encouraged his furry friend. "Go on." He patted him with affection. "Summer doesn't last forever. Enjoy the day."

Strawberry snorted, stomped his left front hoof twice, turned, and swished his reddish-brown tail back and forth while he trotted out the door leading to the pasture. Once he was outside, the uneven clomp-clomping disappeared.

Sam glanced at his worktable and smiled. He looked forward to seeing the look on Esther's face when he gave her his very best work of art. But in order to keep his surprise, the knowledge of the hand-carved present couldn't be shared with anyone.

Except for a spoiled horse who enjoyed sponge cakes. The corners of Sam's mouth lifted into an amused grin.

He returned to his work area and lifted the newly finished piece so it was directly in front of him. While he drew it closer to his chest, he imagined Esther's reaction to it. Because their anniversary was still months away, he'd hide it to ensure it stayed a secret. A warm breeze floated into the wide-open doors and gently caressed his fingers.

For a moment, the barn darkened a notch, but not long after, bright rays poured through the windows. Sam closed his eyes a moment to savor the gentle sensation. But his mind worked while he continued to plan his great surprise.

He straightened and pressed his pointer finger against his chin while he thought. He would write a note to Esther to remind her of his undying love for her. In the message, he'd hint about the present and where it was hidden.

Long strides took him outside where he glimpsed a

jet's trail of white. His gaze eventually landed on the hill and creek behind his home. Annie Mast and Levi Miller had coined the term Pebble Creek to describe the beautiful area. He shoved his hands into his pockets and parted his lips in awe as he marveled at the view.

I love my home. I treasure this land. One of these days, when Esther and I are with the Lord, I don't know who will live here, but I pray that an extension of the Beachy clan will continue to carry on here. God has blessed me with kin, including my brother, who chose the Englisch life. But familie *is* familie, *no matter where they live or what church they go to. And* familie *means love. Just like Pebble Creek.*

Chapter One

What was she doing here? Warm sunlight turned to shade as Jessica neared the front door. She gently let go of her heavy roller bag and two smaller suitcases. Glancing from side to side, she paused to stretch her fingers and proceeded to dig in her handbag's side compartment for the key to Sam Beachy's home.

Smiling in satisfaction, she found the key and lifted her chin with newfound confidence. A breeze moved some loose hairs off of her shoulders, and she sighed in relief. It was a hot June afternoon, and she looked forward to turning on the air the moment she stepped inside.

She bent to unlock her great-uncle's house. When the lock clicked, she slowly opened the door and paused a moment to swallow with sudden unexpected emotion.

As an uncertain knot stuck in her throat, she coached herself to stay calm; yet her heart pumped to a beat that was a combination of excitement and nervousness. Excitement because she had been told the house and the acres that surrounded it would bring a good price after some remodeling. Nervousness because it was necessary to stay here and get it prepared for sale until it was ready to list. Hopefully, that would only take four weeks.

Inside, intense heat made her hair stick to her neck, and she shoved back the thick mass. As she stared at the simple, tidy dwelling, she bit her lip and considered what had transpired over the past several days. So many things contributed to her being here. She was the sole heir to her great-uncle Sam Beachy's estate, way out in the middle of nowhere. That's what it seemed like, anyway. The actual address was Rural Route, Arthur, Illinois. She frowned, continuing to long for a breeze. But there was only a woodsy scent floating through the place.

Remembering her luggage, she pivoted, brought it in, and set her black designer bag in the narrow entrance on a small navy rug. She closed the door and locked it.

To her surprise, there was no dead bolt; Sandy, her real estate agent, had filled her in on this secluded area and insisted it was safe and quiet. Still, Jessica felt more at ease with the door double-locked. In St. Louis, no one was to be trusted. And since childhood, she had constantly watched her back. She'd had good reason to, but quickly forced the bad memories from her mind.

Finally, the disappointing reality set in. *Of course, there's no air. My uncle was Amish.*

She proceeded to the light blue kitchen curtains, pulled them open, and fastened the corners to hooks. She continued to the living room to do the same. Even with sunlight coming in, she figured that the house couldn't get much hotter.

But light made her feel secure. It always had. She brushed away a bead of sweat before it slid down her cheek, then stepped to the side window, where she saw the shiny black buggy parked next to the house. An orange yield sign decorated the back.

Bemused, she stared at the buggy for several long moments before heading outside to get a closer look at what must have been her uncle's only mode of transportation.

She slid open the door of the buggy, stepped up, and took a seat. With great care, she sat on the front deep-blue, velvety-looking bench and glimpsed the small windows. Folded neatly beside her was a homemade knit blanket that resembled the covering on the sofa.

She took in the path that extended from the side door of Sam's house to the back. A different, wider path extended all the way to the barn. She viewed pastures on both sides and could barely glimpse a man standing on a narrow, wheeled platform, being pulled by four horses. She observed the team with interest, realizing that since the Amish didn't drive vehicles, they most likely didn't use tractors, either.

As the sun disappeared behind large, fluffy clouds, the light wind made the buggy creak. Her curious mind traveled at lightning speed as she imagined going places by horse and buggy instead of sitting behind the wheel of her new white Chevy Cruz.

The sun reappeared, and a tree branch moved gently against the buggy. She straightened, turned, and faced the modest-looking home, tapped the toe of her high-heeled pump against the floor, and scrutinized the dwelling.

Grateful that she didn't have to hitch a horse to get around, she closed her eyes and pressed her lips together. *I am here. There's nothing to worry about, really. It's just different than what I'm used to.*

When she opened her lids, she realized that she could charge her cell phone in her car. She could brew tea on the propane stove, but she preferred sun tea. She thought of Sam Beachy and wondered about all the daily tasks he performed without electricity.

Jessica knew she was too curious about other's lives. She tried not to appear nosy, but interesting people intrigued her. She figured that Sam deserved her full attention. *What did I do to deserve such generosity? Uncle Sam, what were you like?*

A couple of hours later, Jessica answered the knock on the door.

A fit-looking man of taller than medium height extended his hand, and she shook it.

"Eli Miller."

"Jessica Beachy."

A rough callus caressed her palm. Of course, his hands wouldn't be smooth, working on houses all day. She also noted his suspenders, crisp shirt, and rolled up sleeves, revealing a set of strong forearms.

A boy who looked to be about sixteen years of age, stepped forward to join them. Eli turned and motioned. "This is my brother, Wayne."

Jessica shook hands again.

"*Wie bist du heit.*"

Jessica assumed he was saying *Nice to meet you.* His grip wasn't quite as firm or confident. But the smile that met hers was every bit as friendly as his older sibling's. Of course, his fingers were rough, too.

"Thanks for making it here on such short notice. You come highly recommended."

With an inviting wave, she motioned them in and shut the door. As they followed her into the kitchen, she grabbed a pad of paper from the tiled countertop and looked at it a few moments before meeting their curious gazes.

"I haven't been here long, but I've managed to jot down some things that need doing to the kitchen." She looked at the wooden floors that stretched to two open rooms. "Of course, you're the professionals, so I'm eager to get your input."

Eli took the paper from her and regarded it as Wayne made his way outside. His gaze drifted to her new book of crossword puzzles on the table.

She smiled a little. "They're my sport."

As he nodded and regarded her list, she took advantage of the opportunity to study him more carefully. He was ruggedly handsome. She noted a light scar on his neck, dark hazel eyes, tanned face, and his taller-than-average build.

Looking back at her, he returned the smile and said, "By the way, welcome to Arthur."

She tried not to grin in amusement. She'd not been here long, but she already knew that the town was much too small for her, and too quiet. She looked around and took in the sparseness of the room—the few pieces of furniture. No pictures. No phone. A delicate-looking blanket in soft blue covered one end of the couch. A jacket hung from a peg on the wall, while a pair of large, worn black shoes rested neatly on the edge of the door-mat. As she considered the Plain Faith, she found herself curious about the people who were so disciplined and tied to their faith as to not use electricity or drive cars.

Eli's voice broke her thoughts. "Where are you from?"

Jessica returned her gaze to him. "St. Louis, Missouri."

When he didn't say more, she went on. "There hasn't really been much time to digest all of this in . . ." She made a wide motion with her hands. "The moment I learned that Sam's four sons had already passed and that I was the single heir to my great-uncle's estate, I got time off of work, packed, and drove here." Fortunately, she had a small check coming in from last year's unused vacation days at her job as a check-in clerk at a hotel. She'd miss the extra money she made from waitressing part-time.

Suddenly, she wanted to explain. She wasn't sure why. "I'm the only child of an only child. When my folks were alive, Sam Beachy was mentioned on rare occasions. Sam's brother, who was my grandfather on Dad's side, never joined the Amish church."

Eli's voice was soft. "Poor Old Sam came down with pneumonia several months ago." He lifted his chin as if he'd remembered something. "By the way, I want you to know that there's no need to worry about animals on the property. Neighbors found good homes for his horse and dog."

"Thanks for letting me know. I can't imagine the amount of work that goes into hitching a horse to the carriage. And the maintenance. Isn't it costly to feed them?"

An amused smile curved the corners of his lips. He nodded. "*Jah*. But they're a necessity. We Amish rely heavily on animals, especially horses."

Her eyes widened. "Until now, I've never known anyone who even owned one. But I've seen plenty of them at night in the city when people take horse-drawn carriage rides. However, that's for pleasure."

"We use them to work and for travel."

She motioned. "Can I show you something?"

"*Jah.*"

Wayne reentered with what appeared to be a tool box as Jessica led Eli outside to the back yard, where tall trees hovered. Leaves danced with the light breeze. She motioned to the pasture that was encompassed by a wire fence, and the huge old red building in the near distance. "The barn needs a fresh coat of paint." Then she turned to face the large tank next to the side of the house.

As if reading her thoughts, Eli offered, "We use propane gas for stoves, refrigerators, and water heaters. And the Amish who live close enough to town can tap into natural gas."

As she took in the acres of farmland that seemed to go on and on, she spoke in a soft voice filled with wonder. "The property's absolutely beautiful. In fact, it reminds me of a fairy tale."

He nodded in silence.

"During my drive here, I saw quite a bit, but what's unique about this place is the hill." She arched an amused brow. "It seems out of place."

Eli nodded in agreement. "It is unusual. Because Central Illinois is predominantly flat." He grinned. "I guess you're right. About the hill being a bit out of place."

Suddenly, pent-up emotion overcame her, and her voice cracked. "I never knew my great-uncle, and he left me this house and beautiful property."

She teared up and lifted her hands in the air before dropping them to her sides. "I don't know why I'm so emotional when I think about him."

Jessica was quick to notice the moisture that sparkled on Eli Miller's eyes. She could glimpse Wayne through the small kitchen window, unloading something. "There was no better man than Old Sam." Eli smiled a little. "And don't worry. I'm going to make sure you're well taken care of."

His words prompted her to sigh in relief. But the soft, mesmerizing way he'd assured her, along with his hazel eyes, made her pulse pick up to a speed that she was sure must be illegal.

Inside the Beachy house, Eli considered the new owner of Sam's home, who looked to be in her early twenties. Honey-blond hair with long bangs framed a lovely set of green eyes. Even though the Amish focused on a person's inner beauty, he couldn't help but think that this girl in her nice, conservative dress and high heels was pretty.

As Eli and Wayne measured the countertops, Jessica's soft voice floated over from the kitchen table where she sat. "Sandy, my real estate agent, told me that your father's the best builder around and that you're following in his footsteps."

Eli turned to offer her a small nod of appreciation before continuing what he was doing. "I don't know about that, but *denki*." He glimpsed suitcases against the wall. Wayne stepped outside while Eli made his way to the table and pulled out a chair across from Jessica. He breathed in the light flowery perfume that hovered in the air. He smiled a little, noting how very different that scent was from the woodsy smell of Old Sam.

A few minutes later, Wayne returned with a handful of things, including a metal tape measure. Eli nodded to his brother. "Go ahead and confirm those measurements on the countertop. Looks like it'll be coming out."

He returned his focus to Jessica and offered his most reassuring voice. "Wayne will help me get your place fixed up."

Eli scooted closer to the table and adjusted in his seat for a more comfortable position. Without warning, an odd sensation swept up his spine and landed at the base of his neck. He rolled his shoulders to rid himself of the uncomfortable tenseness. The feeling had nothing to do with being so close to Jessica. Or hearing her kind, gentle voice.

On the contrary, it was because of who wasn't there. Old Sam. As reality hit him, Eli swallowed an emotional knot that obstructed his throat. He pressed his lips together as he thought through the situation.

He'd been here many times. At Old Sam Beachy's. But now things were different. Much different. This was the first time he'd been here without the hope-chest maker. A sad breath escaped him.

Remembering his purpose, he glanced at the woman across from him and tried a polite smile. But as he did so, reality continued to sink in. It was no longer Old Sam's place. Even the favorite oak chair that he sat on belonged to the new owner.

And although he'd heard that there was an Englisch niece from out-of-state, he hadn't known exactly what to expect. He still wasn't sure. But he wondered how she could walk in such high heels.

As Jessica shuffled through some loose papers, Eli recalled the recent funeral of his dear friend. A pencil made a light noise as it hit the wood floor. As Jessica bent to pick it up, it was impossible not to notice the slender curve of her waist. He forced his attention on the former owner of Pebble Creek, and the corners of his lips lifted.

Hundreds of people had come to pay homage to the most well-respected man around. Eli's family was still receiving cards of sympathy.

As Jessica's gaze connected with his, she asked, "Have you lived here all your life?"

For some reason, the question surprised him. He paused as she eyed the oak chairs that Old Sam had made long before Eli was born.

She extended her arm across the table to hand him her notes. As he retrieved them, he took in her plum-colored nails, considered the simple, reasonable question and nodded. "*Jah.* In the same house."

He nodded. "For nearly twenty years."

Then he skimmed her list and tapped the toe of his boot against the wood floor while a long silence ensued. He focused on what was in front of him, gently strumming his finger against the white papers. Finally, he waved the top page in the air and locked gazes with hers. He arched a doubtful brow.

But before he could speak, a soft, anxious voice interrupted what he was about to say. "How long do you think it will take to do the work?"

Her innocent question prompted a chuckle from his throat. Not because the question was humorous, but because the jobs couldn't possibly be accomplished overnight. The to-do list might be short, but some tasks were time-consuming.

But when he started to explain, the hopeful expression that filled her eyes was so sincere, he forced a smile and tried to ascertain how to best explain. It didn't take long to decide on a simple and realistic approach.

One thing he'd learned from his *daed* was to never be overoptimistic with a customer. In carpentry, the unexpected could occur. Things happened to push back the finish date. Setbacks that weren't anticipated.

Without a doubt, it was far better to offer the most conservative prediction. As Old Sam had always said, "Prepare for the worst and hope for the best."

His *daed* referred to it as taking a precautionary measure and had always stressed how it was better to finish earlier than planned than later.

Eli offered a reassuring nod. "There's good news and bad."

Pausing to lean forward in her chair, she looked at him with an eager expression.

He lowered the pitch of his voice for emphasis. "All this can be done, no doubt about it, ma'am."

"Jessica."

"Jessica," he corrected. "But projects of this size . . ." He hesitated while giving the list another glance. "They take time. One thing I learned from Old Sam was to put out my best quality work, not to rush workmanship centered around detail."

Her eyes widened with interest. "My great-uncle said that?"

Eli nodded. "He was a perfectionist. Especially with the hope chests he designed for people all over the US."

"Okay. So how long are we talking?"

As if realizing she'd said something wrong, she immediately straightened and cleared her throat. "I'm sorry . . . I didn't mean to sound abrupt. It's just tha—"

He looked at her to continue. When the tape measure snapped closed, Eli glanced at his brother. "Better get some numbers on those cabinets, too."

"*Jah.*"

Finally, she lifted her palms in a helpless gesture. "It's just that . . . I'd like the house looking good in a month." She looked away before turning back to him. "I'm taking a few weeks off work to get this place salable. Then I'll place it on the market. And head back to St. Louis."

Her surprising words stopped his thoughts, and he straightened. *List the property? The place he and his family and friends had fallen in love with over the years and considered a large part of their lives?*

Eli decided on direct honesty. "You must be aware that this isn't just any parcel. It's Pebble Creek."

"I thought . . ."

Eli waved a hand. "Pebble Creek isn't the real name; it's what my parents call it. When they were young, they used to meet here. It's where they fell in love. In fact, my *daed* asked Maemm to marry him there. They carried flat stones all the way up to the top of the hill, to sit on."

"It really must be a special place."

Eli nodded.

Several heartbeats later, she softened her voice and asked, "Is something wrong? The look in your eyes . . . Are you okay?"

He nodded. "Of course, the house is yours to do with as you please. I just assumed you were hiring us to remodel so you could live here."

After a slight hesitation, he gave a conciliatory shrug and frowned. "I guess I never considered that it would go on the market."

Breathing in, she nodded acceptance and crossed her

hands over her thighs. Her voice remained calm and logical. "That's my plan." She grinned, and for a moment he thought she was going to laugh.

"What's so funny?"

A bright ray of sunshine floated in and lightened the green shade of her eyes a notch. When he realized he was staring, he looked away in embarrassment.

"Eli, I have to be honest." Her facial muscles seemed to relax a little and she sat back into her chair. "I'm new to all of this, and if I seem a bit edgy, I apologize." She lifted her shoulders in an apologetic gesture. "I'm a bit uncomfortable."

He waited for her to continue.

"It's my first time in the country. I just got here, but already I can tell that it's way different than what I'm used to. It's so quiet. And on my way here, I hardly saw any stores. Or restaurants."

He grinned at her accurate observation. Before he could get a word in, she went on. "All I know is city life. In my ninth-floor apartment, I'm used to hearing music from the neighbors' radios. Traffic. An occasional ambulance or fire truck siren. When I look down from my window, I see cars upon cars."

His jaw dropped as he listened. *She must be glad for the change.*

"Eli, please don't take this the wrong way. I'm grateful for this." She looked around before meeting his gaze. "I want to learn everything I can about my dear great-uncle. It's just that . . . If the truth be known, I feel like a fish out of water. I mean, there's no air-conditioner. No TV." She continued with a small shrug. "No electricity."

She lowered her lids a moment before focusing again on his face. "I don't mean to sound disrespectful, that's the last thing I want." She looked down before meeting his gaze with a curious intensity. "How do you live like this?"

Inside, he chuckled. Now he better understood her. She was out of her comfort zone. A city person who couldn't in the least comprehend how her great-uncle had survived without electricity. A dressed-up girl who believed she'd have time for crosswords. Finally, he couldn't suppress his laugh. To his surprise, she joined in the laughter.

Several heartbeats later, Jessica sighed. "Here I am talking you to death when there's so much to do. Maybe I should just seal my lips and help you get started?" She ran a finger across her mouth.

Eli grinned in amusement. Again, he glanced at the list. "I can give you a rough estimate. But first, I need some clarification." He stood and moved into the kitchen.

She followed him. "Sure."

He raised a brow and pointed to the partial wall that stood between the kitchen and dining room. "First of all, you want this out, right?"

She nodded. "Yes. To open up the area."

He motioned to the fireplace in the dining room. "And you'd like to change the brick?"

"It looks dirty. Is there any way we could have it cleaned to avoid the cost of replacing it?"

He stepped closer to the fireplace and ran a hand over the stonework. "We can do a wash on it to give it a fresh new look. And if that does the job, it's a whole lot cheaper than tearing it down and starting from scratch."

"Good. Then let's try that."

"Okay." He went to the cabinets.

"And you want all new cabinets?"

She pressed her lips together while she ran a finger

over one of the edges. "What I'd like is something more cream-colored. To lighten the room," she added. "These are so dark. And new handles. Maybe brass?"

"I have a suggestion." He tapped his foot to an anxious beat while he thought about how to best serve her needs. "A good friend of mine might be able to redo your cabinets for you. He's highly skilled. And it would save you a bundle of money."

She offered an anxious nod.

Eli frowned. "The only thing is, he's in high demand. I'd have to ask him if he could get them done within your time frame."

"Would you?"

Eli nodded. "I'll ask him at church, but there's no guarantee he'll be able to meet your deadline. But let's check before we think about brand-new cabinets. Because even if you go that route, we're definitely talking about more than a month to get them done and installed."

She lifted her palms and nodded approval. "Okay. Hopefully, your friend will have time to refinish them."

Eli jotted down a note to remind him to talk to William Conrad. After he did so, he glanced at her list before turning his attention to the wood floor.

When he looked up at her, he asked, "So you want to replace the wood flooring with tile?"

"I think so. And the countertop. Between the flooring, cabinets, countertop, and taking this wall out, I think the room will look a lot lighter. Don't you agree?" She snapped her fingers in recollection. "Oh, and I'll pick out new gas appliances. But my real estate agent suggested wiring for electricity . . . to increase my chances of selling."

He took in the drastic changes before offering a simple nod. "The changes you've mentioned will give the room a whole different appearance." He glanced out the window and frowned.

Following his gaze, Jessica motioned outside. "I was going to ask you about that. It looks like that tree's about to fall on the house. Do you think it will?"

He motioned. "Let's have a look."

Outside, Eli and Jessica stepped to the tall oak in question. Eli enjoyed the gentle caress of breeze at the back of his neck. It was a sharp contrast to the hot stuffiness inside. He knocked on the bark, then he went around to the other side and did the same thing.

He stopped to look at her and put a hand on his hip. "It's hollow. It'll have to come down. Old Sam had planned to do it, but with the pneumonia, it just never got done."

Eli continued eyeing the large oak. "I know someone who can take care of this." He jotted on his notepad before returning his hand to his hip. "Anything else?"

When she didn't respond, he glimpsed at her list before tapping his finger against the paper, noticing a couple of additional items. "Besides a fresh coat of paint and a new window above the sink?"

"I think, for right now, that's about it," she said in a serious tone. "I know this is a total makeover of the kitchen. How much will all this cost?"

He motioned to the side door. "How 'bout we go back inside and Wayne and I will do a rough figure? Generally speaking, there'll be a price for materials and labor. Of course, I'll have to check with Mr. Conrad about reworking your cabinets. And without you picking out the window, tile, and countertop, I can only give a general estimate. I'm assuming you'll want to choose the colors?"

She nodded while reclaiming her seat. Her beautiful

eyes claimed his attention. The color reminded him of the grass after a good rain.

Long, thick, wavy hair cascaded over her shoulders and down the front of her sleeveless navy top. And her smile . . . *You're being ridiculous.* Eli silently chastised himself and pretended to force his attention to the list.

"While you're doing that, could I get you a sun tea?" As she slid her chair away from the table, the legs brushed the wooden floor with a light squeak.

She went on. "I stuck a pitcher of water with tea bags in it outside as soon as I got here." She smiled a little. "It should be ready now. Would you care for a glass?"

Thankful for the interruption, he relaxed. Of course, he couldn't blame himself for his reaction to this pretty girl who couldn't imagine life without a television.

"Sure."

When she got up, he pulled his hand calculator from his pocket. His gaze followed her to the back door. The moment he heard the handle click, light summer sounds from the outside floated in. Birds chirping. The gentle lull of the breeze, and oak branches that occasionally brushed the house.

He used the time away from her to gather his thoughts and silently chastise himself. *Stop!*

Recalling his purpose, he quickly regrouped and focused on what needed to be done.

Wayne pulled up a chair next to him. "So the cabinets are coming out. Does she want to stay with oak?"

The door closed, and Eli looked up as Jessica entered with a glass pitcher in her hands. A piece of plastic covered the top. She faced the refrigerator. Her gaze drifted over the large door before she opened the freezer. She closed it and faced them with an amused smile.

"Sorry. There's no ice maker. And no trays of cubes, either. Can you drink it warm?"

He grinned. "Not a problem."

"Wayne?"

"*Jah. Sicher.*"

As Eli estimated material costs and labor, he could hear the clinking of glasses against the tile countertop. A bead of sweat started down his forehead, and he caught it with his hand. *Old Sam had a fan. I've got to find it.*

He turned to his brother. "You want to work on this while I go get us some air?"

A quick nod followed. Eli focused his attention on Jessica. "Before we do anything else, let's cool this place down."

"But—"

"Old Sam kept his fan in the barn. I'm surprised it isn't in the house. 'Course, the weather's been unusually cool till now."

"But there's no electricity."

Eli winked. "Battery."

Chapter Two

Jessica walked ahead of Eli before he moved up to walk at her side on the old winding path that led to the barn. They passed Eli's buggy, which was parked next to Sam's. Eli's horse was tied to the nearby post and let out a loud whinny. When Jessica glanced toward the noise, the horse repeated the sound. In front of her, two monarch butterflies fluttered. In the distance, blades of tall green weeds in the pasture dipped with the light breeze.

Today, the heat seemed like more of a comforting cotton blanket than something to escape. The warm breeze fanned Jessica's eyelashes.

As they continued to the barn to get the fan, and so she could see where her uncle had made his famous hope chests, the creek became more visible. Jessica's pulse slowed to an easy pace. Her shoulders relaxed as she focused on the view. She parted her lips in awe.

"It's more beautiful than anything I've ever seen." She motioned with her hand.

Next to her, Eli spoke in a low, appreciative voice.

"*Jah*. Peaceful, isn't it? And it's something only God can create. His miracles are everywhere."

Jessica pressed her lips together thoughtfully while contemplating his words. She'd never thought of how such a view came about. Was it indeed a miracle?

She wasn't sure. When Eli stopped and turned to her, she immediately stopped, too, and realized that he awaited a response. She couldn't confirm or deny his theory, so she said what she was sure of.

"It's so serene. It really makes you forget your worries."

They continued ahead. Eli didn't respond. But it was okay. The silence between them was nice, in a comforting sort of way. She couldn't talk about God or anything else that she didn't know about. Why try to guess?

As her mind drifted, the path dipped, and she began to lose her balance.

"Oh!"

As her ankles gave way, Eli quickly grabbed her wrist to steady her. Her automatic reaction was a surprised laugh. "That'll teach me to daydream." Seconds later, he dropped his hand, and she thanked him. Still, she found it difficult to focus when she missed the reassuring touch.

What was wrong with her? She silently scolded herself. She reasoned that being out of her comfort zone was definitely getting to her.

I'm independent. I've learned to roll with the punches, and I will adapt to this environment that's very different from what I'm accustomed to. Yes, I'm here by myself. But it's no different than being in the city, really. I'm alone there, too. The main difference is what's around me.

After thinking through her emotions, she lifted her

chin a notch with a newfound confidence. When he glanced down at her, she looked up and smiled.

As they neared the old barn, the air began to smell of an odd combination of woods. They stopped at the gate, and Eli moved in front of her to unbar the large wooden doors. After shoving them open, they stepped inside and looked at each other.

"If you want to know all about your uncle, this is definitely the place to start."

Before she could reply, he continued.

"Ya see, Old Sam spent the large part of his days in here. He always owned a horse. And a dog until shortly before he joined the Lord in heaven. 'Course, the last few months, he passed most of his time in bed."

Jessica frowned. She'd never had a conversation with anyone like this. And she'd certainly never given much thought to where her uncle was now. Joined the Lord? Did Eli really believe that?

Eli looked down at her as if awaiting a response, so she said the first thing that came to her mind. "But you and your family took care of him?"

"*Jah.* But not only us. Our entire church." Jessica's heart warmed at the noticeable affection in Eli's voice. She already felt a strong bond with this handsome, dark-haired Amish man. She didn't know him well, of course, but she could tell that he was protective of Old Sam. Probably of everyone he loved.

"We Amish look out for each other, Jessica. Materialistically speaking, I suppose we don't have a lot. But what we do have is very important. We're a close-knit group." He winked. "Held together by love."

His eyes lit up as he spoke, and she smiled in reaction.

"When one of us is in need, we pool our resources to

cover the cost. Maemm and some church ladies took turns bringing food, keeping the house tidy, and making sure he took his meds and such. The doc, well, he said pneumonia was a tough fight. 'Course, we knew that. Especially at Sam's age. But all through the battle, I never heard your uncle complain."

"No?"

Eli's eyes glistened with moisture. He shook his head.

Jessica swallowed an emotional knot and considered the statement. Already she was thinking of Sam Beachy as someone extremely special. As someone she'd want to know.

Inside, the barn smelled of grain, but as the light, warm breeze floated in through the open doors, an ambience that Jessica had never experienced made her breathe in with satisfaction.

She looked around. To her surprise, it wasn't dark, as she'd imagined it would be. Skylights and large windows allowed plenty of sunlight in. Of course, her uncle wouldn't have been able to do his intricate carving in the dark.

Eli ran a hand over one of the water troughs and stopped to glance at her. "Here's the horse stall." Eli chuckled. "Maemm told me that when Sam's wife, Esther, was alive, she used to name their animals. She even fed the horses sponge cakes."

Jessica laughed. "Really?"

Eli nodded. "'Course, when I was born, she'd already passed. But I feel so very privileged to have been a part of your great-uncle's life. Knowing his beloved wife, Esther, certainly would have been a great blessing, too, but we can never have everything, ya know."

Several heartbeats later, she agreed.

"I'm thankful for what I've had. It's *gut*."

Jessica quickly decided she liked the way he looked at things. As she considered his theory, she realized something that nearly took her breath away. She recognized how very special this man in front of her was.

Somehow, he'd already managed to make her feel welcome and comfortable. His soft, low voice was so convincing. Sincere. She'd never met anyone like him. And she was sure she never would.

Bright sunlight coming in through the skylights made Jessica blink. She hugged her hands to her hips and looked around while Eli made his way to the side wall.

She used the break from him to gather her thoughts. To compose herself. She'd never been the emotional type. Before coming here, she'd viewed things in black and white. Why on earth was her heart pumping at a runner's pace?

As she contemplated the potent question, she watched Eli. Finally, she figured that her emotional state must be the result of everything finally sinking in. The death of the relative she'd never met. Her surprise inheritance. The fact that this was the opportunity she hadn't planned on to buy a home close to work. In a safe neighborhood.

She closed her eyes a moment. Getting rid of the long, busy drive across the city would eliminate most of her stress. She shoved out a shaky breath and straightened her shoulders. *There. It's okay.* As Eli made his way toward her, she smiled and focused on putting things into perspective.

She was in a special place. This wasn't just any barn. No. This particular building was the very place where her dear uncle had created magnificent hope chests for people all over the United States. Special works of art with significant meaning, which he carved so brilliantly. Her real estate agent had gone on and on about his talent.

When Eli rejoined her, she looked down at her shoes as a yearning washed over her. "Eli, I have so many questions I need to ask him." She flung her hands in the air in a helpless gesture. "If only I could sit down with him right now and talk."

The expression that crossed Eli's face was so sincere and genuine, she teared up. "But I can't."

A long, thoughtful silence ensued before she said the only thing that came into her head. "I hope he's in a better place."

Eli's stunned expression caused her to draw in a surprised breath.

"Of course, he is, Jessica. He's in heaven."

The statement came out so honestly and earnestly, like Eli was sure. She continued to study the sincerity in his eyes. "You really think that, don't you?" She searched his face for an expression, but his eyes were unreadable.

"You don't?"

She gave an honest shake of her head. "When my parents were alive, they never went to church. I've never gone, either. I don't think they believed in God. In fact, I'm not sure He exists." She shrugged. A nervous laugh escaped her throat. "How can you be certain?"

She took in the stunned expression on Eli's face. It was as if he'd never been posed the question. But her curiosity came from her heart. It was an honest question. And if he believed in heaven, he could surely tell her why.

Jessica waited for an answer. She'd always wondered how people could believe in something they'd never seen.

When he spoke, his voice was edged with compassion and conviction.

"Jessica, there's a God who loves you. Old Sam knew Him. In fact, I believe that's where he got his wisdom. Near the end, we talked a lot about eternal life, the two of us. That he'd be with Esther and his four sons. And that he looked forward to seeing them and meeting God in person. Our Lord and Savior is why we're here."

Eli turned and began to step away. "Go ahead." He motioned. "Look around while I find the fan. It must be on the other side." He offered a quick wave of his hand and turned to her before stepping away. "Oh, see that?"

She followed his arm to the upper loft.

She nodded.

"There's a window up in the hayloft that offers the most beautiful view of Pebble Creek you'll ever see."

As she listened to his footsteps eventually disappear, Jessica made her way to a workbench in the center of the large structure. Immediately, she was sure that this was where her uncle had created his famous art.

She took in the two chairs, one in front of the bench, and another on the opposite side. Displayed on the bench was a beautiful piece of wood with the beginnings of a design.

She stepped closer for a better look and claimed the wooden chair in front. She traced her finger over what looked like the start of three separate trees. As she leaned closer, she took in the great detail of the bark and the limbs and parted her lips in awe.

To her amazement, the depiction looked real. Old Sam had made the bark look uneven. She imagined how very talented he must have been to have done something like this.

As she stared in astonishment at the work her great-uncle had begun, she found herself giving great thought to Eli's comment about Old Sam having known God and that the hope-chest creator was now in heaven.

The way his words had come out was as significant as what he'd said, as if Eli knew them, without a doubt, to be true. As she touched the detailed carving, she dared to imagine a God and a heaven.

An amused grin followed. The picture she'd conjured up in her head reminded her of a story a parent would tell their child before bedtime. And the ending, of course, would leave the little one with a smile. But Eli hadn't directly answered her question. *How does he know there's really a God?*

Approaching footsteps brought her back to reality. But for some reason, the concept of God and heaven stayed with her. Her curiosity was piqued. As she looked up, Eli grinned.

"I found the fan. It's near the entrance. It's large, so I'll grab it on the way out."

All of a sudden, a squirrel scurried in between them, meeting Jessica's shoes. She glanced down before doing a second take. "He's tame?"

Eli chuckled. "You could say that. Old Sam fed him well, even bought him pecans, and as you can see"—Eli chuckled before shoving his hands in his pockets—"the spoiled little guy's not afraid to beg."

Jessica laughed. "Then we'd better feed him." She looked around before meeting Eli's curious gaze. "Where are the snacks?"

Eli motioned to a nearby cabinet. "I'll get them."

A moment later, Eli squatted and offered a treat to the

small animal, who quickly accepted the nut and scurried out the open doors.

She laughed. "So even the squirrels liked Old Sam."

"*Jah*. And trust me, the little *bettler* will be back for more. Don't you worry."

Eli smiled in amusement before his expression turned more serious. "I see you've come across your great-uncle's last project."

In silence, she lowered her eyes to the board on the workbench and with great affection traced her thumb over one of the trees. She looked up at Eli. "They look so . . . real." She lifted her shoulders. "How did he manage to make them appear so alive?"

Eli shrugged while he joined her in studying the details. "That's what made him such a success. When Maemm was young, she used to spend time with him while he worked. She talked to him about things she didn't speak about to anyone else. And while Old Sam carved, he would offer his very best advice."

Jessica raised a curious brow. "I wish Old Sam could've helped me with my problems." She lowered her voice so that it was barely more than a whisper. "That I would've had him to talk to."

Jessica drew in a deep breath and leaned back in the chair. She looked around. The place was tidy. On the walls, rakes, pitchforks, and work tools were hung meticulously.

Suddenly, a larger squirrel darted in through the open door, pivoted, and rushed back outside. Green leaves and twigs blew in with the breeze and made a light rustling sound against the concrete floor.

The corners of her lips dropped a notch. *Uncle Sam, you were so talented. How I wish I'd been close to you.*

"Let's imagine that Old Sam was still alive and he offered to make you a chest."

Jessica beamed at the happy thought.

"What carving would you have wanted on the lid?"

The question made Jessica think. As she considered Eli's inquiry, she strummed her fingers against the bench and breathed in the pleasant scent of oak. Finally, she lifted her chin and sat up straighter, meeting Eli's gaze with a newfound confidence.

She grinned. "A house."

Eli pressed his lips together. "A house?"

She offered an eager nod as he claimed the seat across from her and leaned forward. "What kind?"

She looked off in the distance as she tried to picture it. Her dream home. Finally, she drew in a breath and folded her hands in her lap.

"A place where I don't need dead bolts. Where nothing bad will happen to me if I forget to lock up." After a slight pause, she continued. "I suppose you could say that my childhood wasn't stable. I grew up never knowing what the days would bring. My father . . . he was an alcoholic. When he drank, he became a different person. I was afraid for so long, I developed anxiety from it. I take medicine to help."

After taking a breath, she went on. "Right now, I have a long, stressful drive through the city to get to my job, which doesn't help. Buying a place close to work will be a tremendous relief, not to mention that I'll be in a much safer neighborhood."

She took in the thoughtful expression on Eli's face. Finally, he said, "I'm sorry, Jessica. I had no idea . . ."

She offered a wide smile. "Things will be better after this place sells."

As soon as the words came out of her mouth, she noted the way the corners of Eli's lips dropped several disappointed notches.

A loud, unexpected bang made her jump up out of her chair. She shouted in fear. "Oh!"

She turned at the sound and saw that a sudden gust of wind had blown the heavy doors closed. She drew in a deep breath and clasped her hands over her chest in relief. Her pulse zoomed at a wild beat.

"Hey, it's okay." Eli's large hand on her arm was firm, yet gentle at the same time. He'd been extremely quick to make his way around the bench to her. In both gratitude and fear, she looked up at him. *There's no need to worry. You're safe here. Forget the past. That was a long time ago.*

"Are you all right?" Deep concern edged his voice. She was quick to note how his hands steadied her. His gentle fingers offered her a sense of reassurance. That everything would be okay.

To avoid further discussion about her past, she offered a confident nod. "I feel silly. I mean, letting something so harmless like that scare me."

Without thinking, she interlaced her hands in front of her and forced a half smile. But she shook. Inside, her heart beat at a fast pace that she was sure would win any race.

He moved his hand up her arm to her shoulder. "Are you sure?" Before she could answer, he went on. "You're shaking like a leaf."

She tried to compose herself. "I'm fine. Really."

Inside, she knew she'd lied. She definitely wasn't

okay. But to her surprise, what disturbed her most wasn't the doors slamming. The real crux of her shaking and pounding heart was Eli's gentle, comforting touch combined with the softness in his low voice.

What's wrong with me? When she stepped back, he dropped his arm. But when he did, she immediately missed his warmth. She forced a laugh and tried to make light of what she considered to be a dire situation.

"I apologize for touching you, Jessica. But you were so afraid . . ."

"It's okay, Eli. That I'm a bit out of my comfort zone might be an understatement." She rolled her eyes. "For goodness' sake, what were we talking about?"

As she pressed a finger to her lips and looked down, it came to her. She snapped her fingers and lifted her chin. "Old Sam. And what my hope-chest lid would be, if he'd made me one."

She dropped back into her great-uncle's chair and focused on the work he'd started. She breathed in decisively and met Eli's uncertain gaze with determination to stay calm.

"I'm sure Old Sam would have done his best work for you. And more importantly, I know without a doubt that he'd want you safe and sound."

He took the hand-carved board on the workbench and studied it with interest. As she watched him, she couldn't help but wonder how such strong, callused hands could provide so much tenderness and assurance.

Eli's confident statement tugged at her emotions because she'd never felt so protected in her life. And although she didn't understand the sensation, she relished it. But why was she comforted by his words? Was it because of this unexpected change in her life?

It's not right to yearn for his touch when we've just met. After all, I don't even know this man. My circumstances are making me crave security even more than usual.

Eli's voice pulled her from her reverie. "He'd just started this one."

She redirected her attention to the carving, thankful to divert attention from her out-of-control thoughts.

"It was for a woman who helps run the local nursing home." He paused to arch his brow. "They're wonderful, by the way. I mean, the folks who work at the home. In fact, Amish and Mennonites often stay there after surgery. Englischers, too. It's so much easier to do rehabilitation without going by car or buggy to therapy every day."

"That makes sense."

"Anyway, she has three young daughters. All under the age of ten. And a year ago, all three planted acorns at the same time. Apparently, a contest started to see whose tree would grow the tallest."

He reclaimed the chair on the opposite side, moved it closer to the bench, and strummed his fingers against the edge, extending his legs.

A laugh escaped Jessica's throat. Eli chuckled. "You know how kids are."

"What did their mom tell them? I mean, a lot plays into how a tree grows. Weather, and . . ." She shrugged. "Well, I don't know what else, but there must be other things."

His expression turned serious. "God has control over everything that grows, including us."

She took in the sincerity of his words. They hit her with such ferocity, their power nearly took her breath away. It wasn't because she believed them; rather, it was the genuine conviction with which they came out. She waited for him to continue.

"Anyway, their *maemm* requested a hope chest with three oak trees of different heights. And in ten years, the tallest would win."

"And the prize for the winner?" Before he responded, she cut in with the snap of her fingers. "The hope chest."

Behind Jessica, Eli carried the large fan as they traversed the long, winding path that led to the house. While Eli reflected on their interesting conversation that had taken place in the barn, he took advantage of the opportunity to more carefully study her.

He took note of the confident way she carried herself. It was as if she didn't have a care in the world. She held her head high. Her long hair was tousled by the warm breeze. The sunlight on her hair lightened it a notch, as if the sun had kissed it. A pleasant fragrance followed her. He couldn't pinpoint the scent, but it reminded him of a fresh basket of peaches.

She glanced back at him, and he returned her contagious smile.

"Eli?"

"*Jah?*"

"Thanks for talking to me."

"I didn't do much."

She nodded before turning where the path curved. "Yes, you did. You just don't realize it."

He considered what she'd just said. He wasn't actually sure what he'd done, besides listen. But it must have been significant for her to draw attention to it.

As they walked, he acknowledged that this was the strangest job he'd ever had. In fact, so far, everything about working for Jessica Beachy was off the charts largely because she was the great-niece of Old Sam. He'd never known anyone who'd had such a tumultuous upbringing.

And of course, now that he'd learned that Jessica wasn't a Christian, he knew in his heart that leading her to the Lord was more important than this job or anything he'd ever do. *But how?*

As he switched the fan and the cord to his other hand, his gaze slid down to her heels. He arched a curious brow, wondering how she could walk in them. To him, they looked uncomfortable, but she seemed to move with ease. Like she was used to them. Without thinking, he found himself imagining how she would look with her hair tied back and tucked under a *kapp*. With a long dress and apron.

It will never happen. As he considered the beautiful girl, an unexpected sadness hit him. *How can a person exist without believing in God?* He contemplated how different his own life would be if he didn't count on his Heavenly Father to get him through the day.

Everything he did revolved around his faith and his belief that Jesus had died on the cross for his sins and had risen. *If a person doesn't believe that, how can they get out of bed in the morning?*

An ache filled his chest as he wondered. Suddenly, he realized the severity of his responsibility. He didn't know what God had planned for him, but what if He'd brought Jessica here to turn her life around?

The more he considered this unusual set of circumstances, the more Eli acknowledged the huge responsibility that now fell on his shoulders. How different being a Christian would make in her life.

That's what he thought, anyway. To live without depending on God for guidance and strength was too much for him to even try to imagine.

Eli wasn't fooled by the confidence the girl appeared to exude. He frowned, recalling her reaction to the loud bang as the barn door had slammed shut. The startled look in her eyes. The light rose color in her cheeks had disappeared the moment it happened. For a few moments, her face had blanched. And he could understand why. The poor girl had been traumatized.

He'd never forget how she'd reacted to his hand on her shoulder. He was fully aware that touching a single woman wasn't proper, but he'd had to do something to ease her fear. And he'd done the right thing because she'd calmed down and had thanked him.

But for some reason, touching her had brought on a strange, uncharted new awareness inside of him. He had sensed a bond with her from the moment they met.

And a large part of it had to do with his need to protect Old Sam's great-niece. *I'm only here to help her. So stop making it more than it is.*

As the bright sun slipped behind a large fluffy cloud, Eli pressed his lips together pensively. Between the barn and the house, he frowned. He didn't know this girl well, but even so, he was certain he wanted to help her. *For some reason, this vulnerable girl brings out my protective nature.*

While he took in her long legs and narrow shoulders, he considered her comment about having a safe home. The more he thought about it, the more he considered it an odd one. Not because it wasn't a believable, legitimate want, it was. But what she'd mentioned was something he'd always taken for granted. Because he'd always had it.

As Pebble Creek loomed in the distance, two things made his pulse beat at a disturbed pace. The first was that she obviously didn't have a safe place to call home. Secondly was her doubt that God existed.

The cord got away from him, and he stopped, set the fan down, and took a moment to wind the white piece loosely around his wrist. Shortly after, Jessica stopped, too, and turned around to face him.

"Eli, I'm happy to help carry that."

He smiled.

As if reading his mind, she lifted a brow and hugged her hands to her hips, squaring her shoulders while giving him a challenging expression. "You don't think I can lift it, do you?"

Without responding, he began walking again. She took a step back to be alongside him.

"I'm sure you can. But I'm the chivalrous type." He swatted a dragonfly away from his nose. "What do you think of that?"

She glanced up at him. He noticed that she didn't look directly into his eyes. Her lashes were lowered, an obvious sign of shyness.

Again, his protective instinct took over. There was something about her that made him want to look out for her. At times, she seemed so . . . vulnerable.

She spoke again in a low voice. "I noticed that right away about you, Eli. When you motioned me into the barn. And inside the house when you held out my chair before I sat down. And of course, when you insisted on carrying the fan."

She looked up at him and he met her look with a serious curiosity. Why did he have this strong need to take care of her? Several seconds later, he still wasn't sure.

Inside the Beachy home, Eli proceeded to the hall closet. Several seconds later, he gave the door a light shove to close it and muttered, "No battery. Next trip over, I'll bring one."

"Thank you, Eli." As if remembering something, she straightened, put her hands on her hips, and glanced at Wayne before shifting her attention to Eli. "Would either of you care for more sun tea?"

"That would be nice," Eli replied.

"*Denki*," Wayne added.

While Jessica stepped away, Eli contemplated the girl who'd inherited this special place and the changes in lifestyle that must seem drastic to her. He considered the changes to be made and the hours involved.

But most of all, he thought seriously about the question she'd asked him about God. Her curiosity had Eli thinking. How could he offer her proof that his Savior existed?

While Eli and Wayne discussed Jessica's plans for the house, Eli's thoughts stayed on Old Sam's great-niece. *She will have to adjust to a house without electricity. I'll get her fan going as soon as I get a battery. That will make things nicer for her.*

Of course, I can only do so much, but I'll try my best

to make her feel at home. He smiled a little. *She'll see how friendly everyone here is.*

Jessica refilled their glasses with the brown-colored beverage, stepped to the table and set the drinks on the oak surface. "Here you go." Quick steps took her back to the small countertop, where she picked up a third glass for herself.

After taking a swig, Eli nodded satisfaction and smiled. "This hits the spot."

Her eyes lit up. "Thanks. I drink tea all day. There's nothing like good ol' Lipton."

Eli shoved his chair back and stood. He turned his attention to Jessica. "If you're in a rush to get this place fixed up, we'd better get busy." He grinned, and she returned the smile.

Without saying anything, Wayne made his way to the entryway. The door made a clicking sound as it closed. From the window, Eli could see him looking for something in the buggy.

"Eli . . ."

He looked at her to continue.

She blushed a little and lowered her chin so she wasn't looking directly at him. "Thank you."

He laughed. "For what?"

"You've reassured me. In a way."

He lifted a brow. "I'm not sure what you mean, but I'm glad I could help."

"You have. To be honest, I'm still a little unsettled about all of this. You know, being away from the city for the first time . . . and knowing that someone who didn't even know me, cared enough about me to leave me this." She extended her hands. "It's overwhelming."

After a brief pause, she went on. "At the same time, I

have a huge responsibility to myself to fix this up and get a good price so I can live close to work and where it's safe."

She shrugged. "I'll stop jabbering. But I wanted you to know that you've made me feel welcome. Thank you."

She reclaimed her seat at the table and finished her tea. When Wayne was back in the house, he and Eli talked between themselves, using a handheld calculator, a pen, and a notepad.

Finally, Eli sat down opposite her and leaned forward. "Here's a rough estimate."

He handed her the paper while his brother went to the kitchen and began putting things back into his work box. Her fingers brushed Eli's, but he quickly acknowledged that the excited jump of his pulse didn't have anything to do with Jessica's heart or soul.

As far as he could recall, his reaction was something he'd never experienced. At the same time, he was certain that it didn't mean anything. But could he blame himself for what his pulse did? If he could push a button to slow down its speed, he would.

Satisfied that he'd acknowledged his feelings, that he was merely reacting to a vulnerable female, a girl who needed him, he studied her again while she contemplated the numbers in front of her.

Ei and Wayne talked about how to accomplish what needed to be done. Jessica disappeared to another room while they did so. But her light, flowery perfume lingered in the room. As she stepped away, he could hear the light click of her heels against the wood floor.

The shade of her hair reminded him of leaves turning color in the fall. Her long bangs nearly touched her dark, thick lashes, and her creamy skin was flawless. As he considered Old Sam's great-niece, he wondered why Sam hadn't mentioned her. Jessica Beachy had never once set foot in this town, let alone in this house, while Old Sam had been alive. Eli frowned.

Obviously, she meant something to him if he'd left her all that he owned. Even if she was the only living descendant.

She rejoined them and nodded. "This seems reasonable enough. But you two won't be doing it alone, right? Isn't there a crew?"

Her question prompted the corners of his lips to drop a notch and he shook his head. "Just us two and our driver, Chuck. Of course, he's not here today 'cause we came by buggy."

Eli rubbed his chin, considering her question. "I understand why you're in a hurry to get everything done. That you're taking off work, and that time is of the essence. And if you'd like, there's a large crew I could recommend . . . they'd have the jobs done in much less—"

Before he could finish, she leaned forward and held up a hand to stop him. "I'd prefer you and your brother, since you were so highly recommended."

He nodded.

She poured herself another drink and returned her glass to the table. As she met his look with a smile, her voice took on a much more serious tone. "You knew my great-uncle." She hesitated. "Already, I feel bonded to you for that, Eli."

He lifted a brow.

She gestured with her hands. "You said something earlier. That he recommended you take your time to do quality workmanship."

"*Jah*. I knew him well. In fact, we considered him part of our family." After an emotional breath, he added, "I wish you could have met him."

She quickly nodded in agreement. "Me too, Eli." She took a deep breath and let out a long sigh. "Suddenly, everything's starting to sink in. His death . . . this house . . . all he left me. I apologize if I've been brusque. It's just that I've been a little stressed. And like I told you, I'm out of my comfort zone. But I'm starting to come to my senses. Now that I've met you and we've discussed the fix-ups, I feel like I'm carrying a lighter load. I want to know everything there is to know about Uncle Sam Beachy. Would you tell me something about him?"

"Now?"

"Maybe a story?"

In the entryway, Wayne motioned with a hand. "Ready."

Eli nodded at his sibling. "Go ahead. I'll be out in a few minutes."

Wayne nodded farewell to Jessica. Eli smiled and relaxed against the back of the chair. *Old Sam would have loved this girl. I know it. And she would have loved him.* He cleared his throat and lifted his chin a notch with determination. "Which one? There are so many." He breathed in. "Your great-uncle was one of the most incredible men I've ever met. And I say that with affection. There was something so . . ."

She sat very still with her palms pressed against her thighs.

"By now, I'm sure you're aware of his love for animals."

She nodded.

"He was wise. In fact, people who knew him went to

him for advice. And trust me, they paid close attention to what he said."

"Really?"

"*Jah*. They always respected his opinion."

Eli interlaced his fingers and released them. "He made elaborate hope chests. Lots of them, in fact. It's hard to explain. When you think of a hope chest, you probably think of a plain chest made to hold special things. But your great-uncle . . . as you could see from what he'd started in the barn, he had this unusual talent for etching beautiful designs into the lids."

Eli crossed his legs at the ankles and scooted his chair back a couple inches for more room. He took another swig of tea and slowly returned his glass to the table. "To him, it was all about the story that went into each lid. People would ask him to make special designs for them. Just like the one you saw in the barn."

She strummed her fingers against the table.

He thought about how to better answer her question. There was a lot to do. Wayne was waiting outside; yet, it was important to him that this Englisch woman knew just what a special soul her great-uncle was. It would have meant a lot to Old Sam. And to Eli, too. Because he considered it his responsibility to keep Old Sam's memory alive.

"Things that represented something significant in their lives." He paused to try for the best words to offer an accurate picture of the man he'd loved and respected.

"He accommodated so many people, Jessica. When Maemm used to keep him company while he carved wood, he taught her a lot."

When Jessica's eyes lit up with surprise, a chuckle

escaped him and he continued. "Maybe that's why she's so wise. She made him sponge cakes after his wife, Esther, went to the Lord. Of course, that was years ago."

"So they were close? Your mom and my great-uncle?"

He nodded. While he contemplated the past week and the grief his *familie* had experienced at the loss of his mother's beloved mentor, he blinked at the sting of salty tears before taking a determined breath to maintain his composure. Old Sam's death was so recent, and Eli was still grieving.

"I apologize, Eli. I can tell that you loved my great-uncle. I hear it in your voice. Maybe it's too soon to open up about him. Especially if he was like family to you. Let's wait . . ."

As he watched the curious expression that crossed her face, he knew at that moment that it was more important than ever for him to let her know how very much Old Sam Beachy had meant to the community.

"It's my privilege to share things with you, Jessica. And even more special to have been close to him."

Eli stopped to clear an emotional knot that obstructed his throat. Salty tears stung his eyes. Tearing up wouldn't help him do justice to Old Sam. And the man's legacy was too special to botch up.

He drew in a determined breath and faced Jessica. "When I think of the number of hope chests he made . . ." Eli let out a low whistle. "From all over the United States, folks requested special lids, and interestingly, each person wanted their lid to represent a story. And some—" He shook his head and a smile curved his lips in amusement and fondness. "They would touch your heart, Jessica."

"Did he ever make one for his wife, Esther? I mean, before she died?"

Finally, Eli shrugged. "I'm not sure. I'll ask Maemm."

As Eli looked around, he spotted what appeared to be nice clothes laid over a suitcase just inside of the bedroom.

Her gaze followed his, and he lifted an inquisitive brow.

As if reading his thoughts, she smiled a little. "I love dressing up on my time off. At the hotel I work at, I wear a uniform." She grinned. "There wasn't a place for everything in the bedroom. Apparently, Old Sam didn't have a lot of clothes, and what he had, he hung on a peg."

She sat up straighter and pressed her lips together in a firm line. "But back to Old Sam and Esther." Jessica laughed. "Did you hear that?" Before Eli could answer, she went on with excitement. "I'm already calling him Old Sam!"

Eli quickly scanned his list and smiled. "And it looks like you'll be needing a clothes rod, too."

She grimaced. "Please. And if you don't mind, the sooner the better."

He eyed the pile of dresses and jackets.

She pointed to the paper he held. "Maybe you can help me decide if anything else needs to be done to help sell this home."

Eli's smile slipped at that last statement. He didn't try to hide his disappointment.

"Something's wrong?"

As she eyed him, the expression that crossed her face was a combination of astonishment and concern. A surprised breath escaped her. "You must have cared for my uncle very much."

She went on, leaning forward. For a moment, time seemed to stand still. Those large jade-green eyes . . . they compelled him. Drew him in.

Her voice brought him back to reality, and he straightened.

"I think it's really sweet."

When he waited for her to go on, she fidgeted with her hands. But she didn't continue. A long, uncertain silence ensued, until Eli smiled a little and adjusted to a more comfortable position.

"It's not just the house, it's the entire Pebble Creek." To emphasize his point, he lifted his palms. Her last statement made him truly realize how very little she knew about her great-uncle and his place. *But I have to tell her.*

The corners of his lips lifted another notch. "When my folks were kids, they used to throw pebbles into the creek to see who could make the bigger splash."

Several heartbeats later, her jaw dropped in surprise. "I'm sorry; I think I get how much this place means to you and your parents. But Eli . . . surely you understand why I couldn't just leave my life and start a new one here in the Midwest."

She paused to spread her arms apart. "And I don't really see a problem with my plan to sell. I mean, even if it has a new owner, what's here can't simply just get up and walk away, right?"

He gave a slow shake of his head.

"The land is here to stay. You can look at it the rest of your life, no matter whose name it's in."

Suddenly, he felt ridiculous for trying to explain Pebble Creek's sentimental worth. How could the woman across from him ever understand, when she hadn't even met the kind, gentle man who'd lived here for so many years?

"I think it's really endearing that you have such a big heart, Eli. But as far as such a strong attachment to a place . . ." She sighed and shrugged. "I wouldn't know about that. I've never had one."

Surprise edged his voice. "You've never been attached to a home? To a place?"

After pushing out a small sigh, she shrugged again. "No."

In the background, the sound of chirping came from the sill of the open screened window.

Eli gave a wry grin. "The birds are expecting to be fed."

"What?" She turned to follow his gaze to the kitchen window.

He chuckled. "Old Sam fed them. Even after he came down with pneumonia."

"Oh!" She threw her hands in the air and smiled. "I've only been here a short while, but I can see that I have some big shoes to fill!"

The corners of Eli's mouth dropped into a frown. *While she's here.* He knew next to nothing about Sam Beachy's great-niece, but what he was sure of was how very different she was from him. He loved Pebble Creek and all his memories of this beautiful spot.

But it wasn't just the property that was an emotional magnet. It was his family and Old Sam. They were connected to this parcel, and he couldn't look at the land without seeing everyone who loved it, and who had grown up here.

He leaned forward and rested his elbows against the table. He held his chin up with his palms and used the most logical tone he could. "This is how I see it. When you were a kid, did you ever play connect the dots?"

He straightened and tapped the toe of his boot against the floor while he awaited a response.

She nodded and smiled. "But what does connecting dots have to do with selling Pebble Creek?"

Several heartbeats later, Eli knew how to explain his sentiment for this beautiful property. "When you connect the dots, you don't just see one, right?"

She shrugged. "I suppose not. What are you trying to say?"

He thought a moment about how to make his concept clear to her. "You see all the dots. And that's how it is with Old Sam's house and Pebble Creek. I don't view this property as one dot. On the contrary, I can't think of this memorable home and the land that goes with it without seeing all the other dots." Realizing he'd said it as best he could, he gently lifted his palms and eyed her to make sure she'd understood.

"What other dots?"

"Old Sam, Maemm, Daed, my brothers and sisters, *familie*. Because we've all created memories on Pebble Creek. It's easy to understand, really. Part of us belongs here."

He noted how the corners of her lips fell before she finally pursed them in doubt.

"You want to know something, Eli? I'm not privy to the history that you and your family have, and I won't pretend to be. And obviously, I'm probably not going to see this the way you do." She hesitated before smiling a little. "But that's not all bad, Eli. I try not to dwell on the past. Trust me, it's not a good place to be. I always try to look forward. Change isn't a bad thing. All I know is how beautiful this place will be when you finish with it."

He could feel his cheeks warm. His heart beat a tad too quickly, and his lungs pumped with great difficulty. Looking down, he forced himself to stop his silly reactions. She seemed to have great faith in him. And he hadn't even begun remodeling. What if she was disappointed?

Of course, he shouldn't worry. The city girl opposite him held a far different view than his. Their upbringings hadn't been similar. The environments in which they'd grown up had obviously been different. Still, his strong, loyal connection to Old Sam and the fact that he was speaking to Sam's heir made him care what she knew and how she felt.

And as far as fixing this place up, she obviously had high expectations. Taking credit for something he'd not yet done was jumping the gun. He hadn't even started.

Jessica Beachy might say kind things to him, and she certainly seemed nice enough, but she definitely didn't understand his emotional attachment to Pebble Creek. But why would she? His memories weren't hers.

Jessica Beachy certainly was direct. She'd been up-front about her plans. And she had asked Eli straight out how he knew God existed.

The sale of Pebble Creek and knowing someone who didn't believe in God prompted the corners of Eli's lips to turn down. *Sam Beachy's great-niece says she's out of her comfort zone. What she doesn't realize is how she's put me out of mine.*

Chapter Three

Two hours later, a knock on the door prompted Jessica to look up. She added her last set of shoes to her queue against the bedroom wall and quickly stepped to the front door.

The moment she opened the door, she faced Eli.

Holding a huge battery, he said hello before making his way to the fan. After setting the battery down, he offered a reassuring smile to Jessica. "Now all I have to do is put it in."

Jessica could hear his horse whinny. She glanced out the window to see the beautiful animal tied to a post.

"How 'bout an iced tea, Eli?" She grinned.

He shook his head. "No thanks." He smiled. "But I'll take a rain check." Jessica watched as he pushed a button. The fan blades began to circle, and a few seconds later, their whirl made a light noise. Jessica moved closer to the coolness and turned to Eli.

Without saying anything, he adjusted the air so that it hit her.

"Thank you, Eli."

"My pleasure."

He snapped his fingers as if remembering something. "Oh, there's good news. A lot has happened since I left a couple of hours ago. I spoke with William Conrad, and he's going to put you at the top of his list for the cabinets."

She drew in an appreciative breath as she crossed her arms over her chest. "That's wonderful."

"*Jah*. It is. He's got a list a mile long to fill, but I'm not surprised he's giving you special accommodation."

She waited for him to continue.

"He thought the world of your great-uncle, too. And his wife, Rebecca, was especially fond of Old Sam. For years, she had a special spot in his barn to dry her plants. And she'd talk to him for hours. 'Course, Maemm and her friend Rachel . . . she's married to a vet . . . did, too. They were like granddaughters to him."

Eli walked toward the door. Jessica followed him. She wished she could keep him around for a while to talk. Everything he said seemed to have a comforting effect on her. At the same time, she supposed it wasn't proper for him to be alone with a single girl, most especially one who wasn't a member of his faith.

At the entrance, he laid his hand on the handle. Before he turned it, he stopped and turned to face her. "I made another call. First thing tomorrow morning, we're getting the oak tree removed."

Jessica smiled a little. "Good."

"That way, I don't have to worry about it caving in through the roof." He winked. "I don't think Old Sam would want that to happen."

"Thanks so much, Eli."

"See you tomorrow."

After the door clicked shut behind him, she went to the window to glimpse him untying his horse and hitching it to the buggy. The uneven clomp-clomping of the horse's hooves got softer until the sound eventually evaporated. She continued to watch him as his buggy picked up speed.

When he was out of sight, she looked out the back window. As she took in Pebble Creek, her shoulders relaxed. And she imagined Eli's parents walking up the hill and looking down at the water.

She could almost see a young girl with her long dress and *kapp*. She wondered what his mother and father had talked about as they'd made their way up the hill. The romantic side of her imagined them sharing a kiss.

As Pebble Creek loomed in front of her, she pictured herself in Eli's mother's shoes. She wondered what it would feel like to walk hand in hand with a man, next to the creek.

Suddenly, she blinked at the sting of salty tears as her mind drifted to her youth. Her father's loud swear words echoed through her head. She could almost hear him yell. She could nearly see herself running into her bedroom to dodge a beer can thrown at her.

No matter how peaceful-looking Pebble Creek was, she'd never be able to forget the chaos she'd grown up in. She wished she could have assured her mother that everything would be okay. How she yearned to redo her past without an alcoholic father who had repeatedly told her she'd never amount to anything. If only every sound didn't remind her of beer bottles hitting the wall. Of the slapping sound of his palm against her cheek.

As her heart pumped to an uncomfortable speed, she

closed her lids and coached herself to think positive thoughts. That's what she'd gotten from the counselor she'd seen for stress issues.

She breathed in slowly, then breathed out. Her vision of Pebble Creek blurred as tears filled her eyes. Her counselor's words replayed in her head.

Jessica, you can't change what came before today. No matter how hard you try, what's happened already is final. Only you can stop it from making you unhappy. A whole new chapter in your life is waiting. And you can write it. Use the bad experience to help you be a stronger, better person. That's the good thing about the past; whatever it is, you can always learn from it. Use it to your benefit. Focus on the future, Jessica. On everything good. On what you really want out of life. Only then will you find true contentment.

She breathed in and leaned forward with her arms crossed on the windowsill. Pebble Creek inspired her. When she took in the beautiful property, she wanted to create that new chapter that her counselor had encouraged. As the fan made its light whirl, she knew more than ever that she wanted a happy, safe life.

Like Eli Miller had. Of course, he hadn't told her that his life was good, but he didn't have to. She could see it in his eyes. Hear it in his voice. She sensed it in his comforting, reassuring manner.

A loan would cover his services until she paid it off with the money from the sale of the property. But already Eli offered much more than the opportunity to remodel the kitchen. He provided her with hope. When she looked into his eyes, she saw everything good. And in her heart, she wanted a future with someone who loved her and cherished her. A man just like Eli Miller.

The following morning, Eli helped William Conrad carry the last of Jessica Beachy's kitchen cabinets into the large workroom of Conrad Cabinets. On the opposite side, William stopped and counted. "One, two, three." On the third count, they carefully set the last cabinet alongside the others on the cement floor.

Above, large ceiling fans whirled, making a light whistle as a welcome flow of air caressed Eli's neck. William straightened his knees and sighed as he pressed his palms against his work pants.

"Word has it that Old Sam's place is goin' up for sale. A real estate agent mentioned it in town this morning."

Even though Eli was fully aware of the potential sale, he felt an ache in his chest. Would he ever accept that Old Sam's home would be on the market? That anyone could buy Pebble Creek?

William swished his palms against each other to dust off the particles, and went on to press his palms against his hips. After clearing his throat, he lifted a challenging brow. "So the new owner of Old Sam's place . . . she's really going to list it?"

Eli nodded and let out a sigh. "*Jah*."

A soft voice prompted them to turn to the side door, where William's only daughter waved an inviting hand. "Would either of you care for a glass of fresh lemonade?"

Eli nodded appreciation. "I'd love one, Mary." The girl's shyness made him smile. She was a whiz when it came to plants. Already, she had one of the most productive gardens in the area. And she was only sixteen.

Usually she didn't say much until that subject came up. Then her shyness quickly evaporated, and she became a talking plant-encyclopedia. Whenever someone from church had a question about something green, they went to Mary. And as far as creating arrangements, there was nothing she wouldn't try. No one could match her botanical prowess.

"Eli, would you like to see my garden before you leave?"

The light in her eyes told Eli he couldn't disappoint. "I was hoping you'd show it to me."

"After you taste my lemonade." She beamed.

"That's the best offer I've had all day." Eli winked at the girl, who shyly lowered her gaze to her shoes. When she looked up, she turned her attention to the owner of Conrad Cabinets. "Daed?"

"Extra ice in mine."

Eli noted the pink flush of her cheeks. William and Rebecca's daughter would make someone a good wife when she was older. It was common knowledge that the girl did everything to perfection. She'd inherited her *maemm*'s interest in gardening and helped Rebecca with her floral business.

Eli and William focused their attention back on the cabinets. As Eli took in the large room where William worked, the smell of varnish filled his nostrils. Each section of the room seemed to sport a different station.

Drills, hammers, knives, chisels, and different sizes of boards were visible all over the large area. William turned his attention to one of the cabinets and gestured. "Now, what exactly would you like for me to do with these?"

Eli joined him, and they meandered past the row of cabinets they'd set in the side area.

The sound of the door clicking open made them turn again.

"Lemonade." Mary handed the men their drinks with a smile, they thanked her, and she left the shop.

Eli resumed his conversation with William. "Right now, the kitchen's closed in. I'm opening it up to the dining room and trying lighter wood and a more modern design."

Eli went on to explain specifics. A long silence ensued while William assessed what needed to be done. Eli finally broke the silence. "Does that sound doable?"

William patted Eli on his shoulder and smiled. "I'll have these done by next week."

"Sure appreciate it."

"Anything for you." His grin widened, and he added an extra pat to Eli's back. "And for Old Sam."

That evening, Eli washed his hands in the hall bathroom of his home. While he rubbed his soapy palms together, he considered the interesting girl in Old Sam's house and how she'd already challenged his steady, uneventful life. As he used the soft blue hand towel, a voice interrupted his thoughts.

"Eli! Supper's ready!"

Eli straightened the damp hand towel on the hook and stepped to the dining room table, where his mother set a cloth-lined basket in the middle. Eli's stomach growled as he breathed in the delicious smell of homemade yeast rolls.

But that wasn't the only enticing scent. He'd glimpsed the fresh batch of sponge cakes on the kitchen countertop.

His mother was famous in the area for her specialty. And Eli considered himself very fortunate.

He knew Maemm would want to know all about Jessica Beachy, so he wasn't surprised when she broached the subject. While she organized the dishes, he sensed her curiosity to know more about the newcomer.

"Tell me about your day, Eli. I'm dying to hear all about Old Sam's great-niece." As Maemm stepped away to the kitchen, she asked, "What's she like?"

Before he could answer, she went on. "She must have been very special to Old Sam. But in all the years I knew Sam, he never mentioned her."

As Eli pulled out a chair at the dinner table, they all took their usual seats at the table. All five of them. Maemm, Daed, Wayne, John, who'd been named after his *dawdy*, and Eli.

They all bowed as Daed blessed the food. "Amen."

When Eli opened his eyes and lifted his chin, he considered how to tell his folks that Jessica planned to sell Old Sam's Pebble Creek property. As Maemm passed the fresh peas his way, he was fully aware that Jessica's plan would need to be addressed. And now was as good a time as any to break the shocking news to his family. He frowned.

His father spooned a large helping of chicken and dumplings, turning to Wayne and then Eli as he did so. "You must have a lot of news. Looks like we've got ourselves a new neighbor."

Eli was quick to note Wayne's silence, and let out a decisive breath as he regarded his *daed*, who dished up a large helping of garden peas. "There's one thing for sure, Jessica Beachy has a list of fix-ups. She seems nice.

Englisch. Is from St. Louis and it's her first time in the country."

The others looked at him with keen curiosity.

Excitement edged Maemm's voice. "I'll take sponge cakes over to give her a big, warm welcome. And she'll certainly need help getting situated. Maybe I can help her clean."

Eli gave a quick shake of his head. After clearing the knot from his throat, he looked around the table. "I hate to tell you this, but she's gettin' the house all fixed up to sell."

He paused while taking in the jaws dropping around the table. Wayne lowered his gaze to his plate. A long, tense silence ensued. If someone had dropped a fork, the sound of metal meeting the shiny oak floor would have been too loud.

John finally broke the silence. "You surely don't mean she's going to sell Pebble Creek?"

At the same time, Eli's parents stopped eating and looked at each other in dismay. Offering a small nod, Eli faced his mother's worried expression. He softened his voice to a more sympathetic tone. "I'm afraid so. And she's having it wired for electricity . . . just in case the buyer's *Englisch.*"

When his mother smiled a little, he drew in a small breath of relief. His *daed* didn't respond. Eli was quick to note his frown and the tiny creases around his eyes that appeared when he considered something serious.

"You know, your *daed* and I have always considered Pebble Creek ours." A nervous laugh escaped Maemm's throat as she eyed her husband with affection. "From when we were kids, we met there . . . right at Pebble

Creek . . . to talk and throw pebbles into the water to see who could make the bigger splash."

Levi smiled with affection at his wife. "Your mother, I've got to tell you . . . she gave me a run for my money. She had quite an arm."

She gave a gentle roll of her eyes before meeting Eli's gaze. "Your father . . . he's just bein' kind. As you know, I was quite a bit younger than him. And he always seemed so tall."

After taking a drink of water, she returned her glass to the white napkin on the oak table. Ice cubes clinked against her glass. "Did you know that Levi and I even carried stones from the creek-side all the way up to the top of that hill?"

Eli nodded and waited for her to go on.

"It might sound crazy, but we took them several feet at a time. Then we'd set them down and rest." She chuckled. "They were heavy. Finally, we got them to the top and used them to sit on."

Daed talked under his breath while he buttered his hot roll. "We even named the creek. The name . . . it became obvious to both of us."

Several heartbeats later, Maemm's voice was barely audible. "Pebble Creek."

"Annie and I . . . well, we spent as much time together there as we could. We asked permission, of course. Our time together there . . . it never did seem long enough, did it?"

Annie merely offered an affectionate smile. Levi shook his head and swallowed. After finishing off his peas, he met Eli's gaze and smiled. "Your *maemm* and me . . . sometimes our folks would let us go to the creek if we finished our chores early. And then . . . after I came back for the wedding . . . well, you know the story. We started meeting there again. Things were the same, but somehow they were different."

Eli noted the light color filling his mother's already rosy cheeks.

Levi eyed Annie. "It seems like it was yesterday, doesn't it?"

She nodded. "But when you left . . ." She lowered her gaze and waved a dismissive hand. "We won't talk about that. I'm so grateful that Levi decided to come back to his cousin's wedding."

"God guided us to meet again. And"—he looked around the table before sipping his coffee—"God blessed us with a happy ending. Meeting up with your mother after a decade apart . . . now I don't care what you say, that was no coincidence." He cleared his throat and spoke in a more emotional tone. "That's what you call God's hand at work."

Eli watched his mother's eyes glisten with moisture. "*Jah.*"

He loved the expression of love and affection between his father and mother as they drifted back in time. "We had some heartbreaking moments there." Levi's voice cracked. "But at the end of the day, they got resolved. Annie and I . . . when we agreed we couldn't marry because of our difference in faith, we prayed a lot."

"And God rewards the faithful," Annie cut in. "That's what Mamma always told me. But she was right. Because Levi came back to town. Unexpectedly, I might add," she said, addressing her children. "And that very time we met at Pebble Creek was when your father told me he'd join the Amish church and we'd get married."

"Annie . . ." He chuckled lightly. "Ya see, she made the best sponge cakes I'd ever tasted."

Everyone laughed.

"She still does. And she always wanted a happy ending for everything."

Maemm lifted her chin. "I still do."

"And that's why I should have known all along that we'd marry."

"Happy endings are what we all want, right?"

Eli thought about the question before finally nodding agreement. "I guess so."

"Every secret we ever shared was said at Pebble Creek. But there's something else . . ." She breathed in and closed her eyes. When she opened them, her voice was barely audible. "It's where I used to dream. But I wasn't the only one."

She darted a quick, mischievous glance at Levi. "Since we were kids, Levi imagined building a home there."

John lifted a curious brow while he swallowed the last bite of his roll.

Eli stopped eating and digested the statement. He'd always known Pebble Creek was special to his folks; he'd never realized that Daed had dreamed of building there.

He swallowed a bite of chicken and looked at his father with skepticism. "Is it true, Daed? Did you try to buy the land from Old Sam? Did you think he'd sell it to you?"

After a slight hesitation, Levi reached for the casserole dish and spooned more dumplings onto his empty plate. "I never asked him. I'd given it some thought, but I just didn't feel right about it."

He paused to load his plate with more peas. "I mean, if he had sold it to me, where would he have gone? And the last thing I wanted was for him to think we wanted him to move so we could buy his land."

Eli considered his *daed*'s words. And Eli agreed. Asking Old Sam for Pebble Creek, the place he called home, would have been wrong.

"The whole thing . . . I guess it wasn't meant to be. To my knowledge, he didn't ever plan to sell it . . . at least, not as long as he was alive." He grinned.

"But the Lord took care of us."

Levi waved a hand in gratitude. "Annie and I built this beautiful home." He shrugged before going on. "Pebble Creek was always a dream." He paused and then said with emotion, "A dream that never went away."

Eli met his *daed*'s gaze. "But dreams are *gut*, *jah*?"

The response was a slow nod. The corners of Eli's lips dropped as he considered the depth of his parents' attachment to the property that Jessica Beachy now owned. An idea popped into his mind. A long silence ensued before he decided to voice his thought.

"Could we buy it, Daed? I mean, if we all pitched in?"

Wayne and John glanced at each other with a curious intensity until John spoke up.

"The cost of land is sky-high these days. And the part behind Pebble Creek, it's prime."

The senior Miller finally commented, "As much as your idea appeals to me, I don't think we could come close to affording it."

Levi glanced at Annie. "Besides, we'd never even think of leaving this home that we built together after we married. But there's something we can do. We can pray for a nice family to move into Sam's house to make new memories." He grinned before going on. "Kids running around the yard. A mother baking homemade pies in the kitchen. That's what Sam would have wanted."

Finally, Eli's mother offered a smile of agreement. "*Jah.*"

His brothers were quick to add their nods. For some reason, Eli felt the need to assure his mother that Jessica seemed to be a good person. "You know, she's from Missouri, and I kinda understand why she wants to sell."

His mother raised an inquisitive brow and leaned forward in her seat.

Lifting his palms, Eli crossed his legs and then lowered his hands to rest on his thighs, tapping the toe of his shoe while he explained. "I mean, she did inherit the land. I can't really blame her for wanting to sell when she's not even from this area. Her job, her life . . ."

He offered a conciliatory lift of his shoulders and sighed. "They're not here. It would be like us moving to Missouri, I guess."

Maemm's eyes glistened with moisture and her voice wavered. "Of course. I can see why she doesn't plan to live here. It's just that Old Sam . . ." She looked down a moment before glancing around the table. "I can't help but wonder what he would think if he knew she was putting the land up for sale." She followed with a small shrug.

Eli nodded agreement.

With a helpless sigh, she said, "I know it's not my property, and it's really none of my business, but for the life of me, I can't imagine that he would leave it to someone he thought would sell. I won't pretend to know what was going through his mind, especially near the end, but I think I could say with a fair amount of certainty that he intended to keep that land in his family, even if that meant leaving it to a distant relative. That's how he was. Family meant everything to him, even if they weren't close."

For some time, the only sounds were the light clinking of utensils against plates as Eli considered his mother's comments, and thought about the new owner of Pebble Creek.

Levi spoke in a low, thoughtful tone. "Old Sam was wiser than any of us. I know he had never met his great-niece, but I'm sure he knew things about her and her family that we don't."

He added, "Old Sam must have believed that Jessica would live here."

Chapter Four

That evening, Eli stayed on Jessica's mind while she lit the wick of her vanilla candle and took a seat on the living room sofa. Years ago, a counselor had recommended scented aroma for relaxation.

She breathed in the calming smell while she considered everything she'd learned about Old Sam. While she contemplated Eli, she closed her eyes a moment.

Strangely enough, there was something about the Amish builder that comforted and excited her at the same time. How could that be? It was an emotion she'd never experienced.

Her gaze drifted to the fan. As the air blew on her hair, she turned her head to the window that offered a beautiful view of what Eli had referred to as Pebble Creek.

It was her understanding that this wasn't the official name but rather what it had been called for years by his family, dating back to when his parents were kids. As the pleasant scent of vanilla filled the air, the sun began slowly melting into the western sky.

She stood and stepped to the window for a better view. The colors were a mixture of the most beautiful hues she'd ever seen. It was as if an artist had spilled different shades onto a canvas. She let out a sigh of relief. In St. Louis, she'd never really paid attention to sunsets.

But here, out in the middle of nowhere, she couldn't believe she'd never admired the sky before. As the sun continued to dip, the colors became a notch lighter. She couldn't take her eyes off it.

The warm breeze floated in through the open window, moving some loose hairs into her face. She shoved them back over her ears.

She smiled as she admired the beautiful creek. Her mind drifted to the story of Eli's parents, two kids meeting there and falling in love.

Jessica turned and made her way to her open suitcase, where she began unfolding her clothes and looking forward to a clothes rod.

"Old Sam." She shook her head. "We are as different as night and day, yet I still feel so close to you. Why couldn't I have met you?"

She considered the man who'd left her this place and frowned. "I don't even get to thank you."

She began laying her clothes out on the back of the sofa to get rid of the wrinkles. Tomorrow, she'd buy hangers. As she continued to pull things from her suitcase, she couldn't stop thinking about the interesting story about Eli's mother and father, Levi and Annie Miller. Their romance piqued her interest.

As the pleasant scent of vanilla drifted through Old Sam's bedroom, she imagined what the Millers must have gone through. She also wondered what Amish people would do outside of their own community. They obviously wouldn't know how to drive a vehicle. And how could a person who'd belonged to such a close-knit group suddenly adjust to entirely different rules?

Remembering the disapproval on Eli's face as she'd revealed her plan to sell this property made Jessica tense. She pulled her anxiety medicine from her makeup bag. She started to open the bottle, then stopped. Did she really need it?

She glanced at her hands. *They're shaking.* She downed a pill, returned the bottle to the bag, went to the kitchen for a drink of tea, and glanced at her puzzle book on the table. Then she focused on tomorrow, when Eli and Wayne would continue the kitchen makeover.

She stood, hands on her hips, while she pictured how the kitchen would look after they'd done the renovations she was requesting. Even though the house was outdated, she was fully aware that the place had considerable value. Location. Her agent had told her that you could always fix up a house, but that you could never move the lot.

She lit the gas lamp above her head, then returned to the window to watch the sun take its final dip and disappear. She was grateful for gas lighting. It certainly made being without electricity a whole lot more bearable.

I thought I'd be afraid to stay alone in the country. She lifted her chin a notch and smiled. *But so far, so good. Except I wonder what Eli's parents will say when they find out Pebble Creek will soon be on the market?*

She returned to the bedroom, where she turned down the beautiful quilt of blue hues. She slipped on her sweats and T-shirt, and sat on the edge of the bed. Tomorrow she would see Eli again. She'd find out more about her uncle. And about the rugged-looking, dark-haired carpenter.

* * *

Saturday morning, Eli and Wayne helped their *daed* put finishing touches on his newest project. Eli stood at the top of the ladder and carefully dipped his brush into cream-colored latex paint. John was working on another project on the north side of town.

As the cool breeze drifted in through the open windows of the new construction, Wayne came and stood at his side and looked up.

"You mind sharing?"

Without responding, Eli stepped down before reaching for the paint. With great care not to spill, he poured the thick mixture into his brother's plastic bucket while Wayne held the container very still. The scent of latex filled the air.

Their father joined them. "Hey, ready for lunch?"

The two boys nodded simultaneously.

"Let's wash up."

Eli and Wayne proceeded to retrieve the lids to their cans of paint and put them back on. Before stepping outside, they dropped their brushes in the soaking bucket.

Together, they stepped to Levi's work truck, where the senior Miller's driver and coworker, Sherman, joined them. In their community, it was common for the driver to also work with the Amish. Eli and Wayne had their own driver. Behind the truck, Wayne grabbed the release latch, and his *daed* held on to the tailgate so that it would fall gently.

One by one, the four men jumped up into the back. Eli opened the cooler lined with soft white towels, and placed it between him and Wayne. Wayne pulled out one of the Tupperware containers, and handed it to his father.

He gave the next meal to Eli. Then he got his own. They sat on the tailgate. Behind them, Sherman sat on an extra cooler and pulled his own lunch from a paper bag. Eli peeked between the two slices of homemade bread to check what was inside. Wayne beat him.

"My favorite. Sauerkraut and ham."

Levi chimed in. "And no one makes 'em better than my Annie." He turned to Sherman.

"Here. Take half of mine."

Sherman lifted a dismissive hand. "No, no. Thanks for the kind offer, but I'm fine with what I've got."

Levi leaned back to display his meal to his driver. "You sure about that?"

Sherman laughed. "Now, you're really tempting me."

Levi motioned to the cooler. "Go ahead. There's extra."

Sherman finally accepted and thanked him.

A long, comfortable silence passed while a cool breeze caressed them, and they ate.

The cloud-filled sky certainly wasn't a disappointment. The crops could use a good rain. The forecast looked promising, and the air already smelled of moisture.

As Eli downed his sandwich, he glimpsed a horse-drawn buggy in the distance.

The scent of fresh paint floated out of the open windows. A red bird perched on the limb of a small oak that decorated the large front yard of the Schrocks' place. Behind them, landscapers planted a straight line of evergreens that would make a nice border once they filled out.

Eli watched as two workers transported the trees, one at a time, from the back of a blue Ford pickup truck to a row of holes and placed each seedling in its spot. Two Coke cans littered the yard. Eli wondered why they couldn't use a trash bag.

A large sign in front of the house, near the blacktop, advertised Miller Homes. Eli took in the brand-new house his father had built. Without even looking, he knew every detail by heart: the brick archway at the entrance, tiled patio, the bay window in front of the living room.

Eli admired the new place his father had designed and built for an elderly couple who were ready to retire. Daed had drawn up the home according to their wants and needs. In Eli's opinion, it was his best construction to date.

Large pillars stood on each side of the front entryway. The oversized front door arched at the top. His gaze traveled to the roof.

Something about new construction made his heart warm. The thought of a family enjoying the house prompted a smile. He imagined a grandmother cooking homemade dishes, and little ones chasing each other in the large yard.

For a moment, Eli dared to wonder if he'd be a father one day. He was already twenty-three. To his chagrin, the right woman hadn't come along. He'd been told that selecting a mate meant choosing someone he could count on to do the chores. Take care of the kids. A partner he could depend on.

Of course, he knew that marriage was about being there for each other and that physical attraction wasn't necessary. He yearned for a wife with all the qualities he treasured, but shouldn't there be some sort of a spark? Something stronger than friendship and counting on the other person? He hoped he'd find out. Of course, what mattered most to him was growing in Christ with his spouse.

As Daed and Wayne chitchatted with Sherman, Eli imagined a woman he couldn't wait to come home to. Someone he thought about all day. But was his want merely a dream? He shrugged, letting out an uncertain breath.

The couple who would soon move into this beautiful home had four children and seven grandchildren. They had a beautiful life together.

"Someone's awfully quiet." All three gazes traveled to Eli before the elder Miller spoke. "Whatcha thinking?"

Eli waved a dismissive hand. "Ah, it's nothing."

"Yeah, right." Amusement edged Wayne's lips as he glanced at Eli. "He's probably got Old Sam's niece on his mind."

In response, Eli grinned. "She is pretty nice."

Levi cut in after taking a swig of bottled water. "Hey, we haven't talked much about Pebble Creek today. You gonna be able to do the kitchen she wants?"

Eli chuckled. Not because the question was funny. It wasn't. But compared to Jessica not knowing Christ, the kitchen was low on his list of concerns.

"What's so amusing?" His *daed* lifted a curious brow, downing another bite of sandwich.

Eli contemplated his response before he spoke. If he told the truth, the conversation might put Old Sam's niece in a negative light. And that's the last thing he wanted. However, on the upside, his father might have an answer. If Eli didn't broach the subject, he'd never know.

Eli decided to put his thoughts out there. "Daed, something's weighing on my mind. About Jessica."

Levi frowned, crossed his knee and turned to face his sons. Concerned, he asked, "She's not happy with the price?"

Eli hesitated, trying for the right words. "It's not that."

By this time, Wayne had ceased eating and stared at Eli with a raised brow.

"While Jessica and I were in Sam's barn looking for the fan, we had a serious conversation." Eli continued to meet curious glances. He followed with an uncertain shrug. "She doesn't believe, Daed."

A long silence followed while his sibling and father eyed him with disbelief. Finally, Levi broke the silence.

"You mean she doesn't believe in God?"

The potent question prompted an emotional knot in Eli's throat, and he tried to swallow it. He knew the issue was serious, but when he actually heard his words, he realized just how severe the situation was.

He finally shook his head. "No."

Eli watched his brother's jaw drop.

"Now I know why you two were in the barn so long," Wayne said. "I wondered what was up."

Levi's voice was firm. "Wow."

"I know, Daed."

No one said a word. The only sounds were of shovels meeting the earth in the yard and the barely audible voices of the landscapers.

"Eli, to be honest, what you've just said . . . well, you took me by surprise, Sohn. Round here, I've never come across anyone who didn't believe in the Creator of the universe. But this is something we can't ignore. I'll do some serious thinking. And pray. God must have placed Old Sam's great-niece here for a reason. Maybe he gave her to us to help God come into her heart. Now I understand why you laughed at my question 'bout the kitchen. When it comes right down to it, nothing's as important as believin'."

"She seems open-minded. Said she wants to know everything about Old Sam. She loves him . . . she's never said it, but I see it in her eyes. Hear it in her voice when she asks me things about him. It's a shame they never met."

The senior Miller chugged water from his plastic bottle. "That's why we need to treasure every minute here on earth. To do what's important. Tomorrow, we can't redo today."

Eli nodded agreement. "Our conversation surprised me. When she said she hoped Sam was in a good place . . ."

Wayne took a swig of water and coughed. He cleared his throat.

Eli continued. "She doesn't know. I don't think she's convinced there's *not* a God. At the same time, she's not certain there is."

Eli glanced toward his role model. "She asked me flat out how I know God exists." After a slight pause, he asked, "What would you have told her, Daed?" He decided to reword his question. "If you'd been in my shoes, what would you have said?"

Wayne had become unusually quiet. So had Sherman.

"You've got me on that one, Sohn." Levi hesitated. "It's hard to believe that anyone related to Old Sam would doubt God's existence. The man lived by the Bible."

Wayne finally broke the long silence. "The more I think about it, helping her isn't just up to you, Eli. I'll pray, too."

Eli let out a breath and locked gazes with his father. "I know we have to make sure she knows God." He lifted his shoulders in a helpless gesture. "But how do we make her believe?"

* * *

That evening, Eli knelt by his bed and pressed his palms together. The mouthwatering aroma of yeast dough filled the air. He could still taste chicken broth on his lips. As he prepared to talk with his Lord and Savior, he thought of Jessica Beachy and how she needed God in her life.

He squeezed his eyes closed, desperate to know how to get her to know Christ.

"Dear Lord, hear my prayer. You've given me so much, and I thank You for my *familie*, my health, our church, and our friends. But tonight I come to You in need, Lord. Please help me to say the right things to Old Sam's great-niece about Your love for her. That You died so that all of us who believe in You will have eternal life. This is too important to make mistakes. So please fill me with the right words."

He followed with the Lord's Prayer.

"Amen."

The next day, a thoughtful sigh escaped Jessica's throat as she stepped outside, iced tea in hand. The calming vanilla scent from the candle burning on the table filled the air.

The recent changes in her life made her head spin. Old Sam's death. Her inheritance. Her temporary move. Eli. *But now I'm here.*

She walked behind the house and stepped closer to Pebble Creek. Her heart rate slowed to a relaxed beat. She smiled.

Finally, she turned and looked down at the large flower bed beside the home. A buggy wheel perched in the middle of the garden, with green vines intertwining its spokes, creating an interesting visual.

After charging her phone in her car, she'd googled to find out what kind of flowers they were. After learning that they were called black-eyed Susans and coneflowers, she wondered if Old Sam had planted them. *He must have.*

She bent to sniff the light, pleasant-smelling purple centers of the coneflowers. As she touched a fragile-looking leaf, she sorted through her swirling thoughts. She'd hesitated to come to central Illinois. After all, the countryside was a far cry from St. Louis's hustle and bustle.

This small town was a whole new world for her. Eli and his brother dressed differently, talked differently, lived their lives differently. She hadn't been here long, but judging by her interactions with the Millers and what Sandy, her real estate agent, had told her, Old Sam's community was way more conservative than what she was accustomed to.

She lifted an inquisitive brow, sighed, took a drink, and squared her shoulders. She smiled when a monarch butterfly landed on the windowsill. In the distance, a red fox appeared and quickly disappeared. But the field behind the house presented the most interesting view of all: four horses pulled a wheeled platform with a man standing on it.

For several moments, she thoughtfully took in the unique scene, and imagined the physical work to raise crops and make hay as opposed to using machinery. She greatly admired anyone who worked so hard.

Brushing off the distraction, she squared her shoulders and recalled her purpose. Glass in hand, she looked around at what needed to be done and let out a deep sigh. *Time to get to work.* She looked up at the roof. The gutters needed to be cleaned.

Inside, she stepped quickly from room to room, each painted a light blue. Right now, she wasn't sure what to do with the furniture.

She pressed her lips together in deep deliberation. She wasn't ready to part with anything that had been owned by her great-uncle.

She took a quick drink, and the ice clinked as she set her glass on the countertop. She ran her fingers over her forehead, pushing her bangs out of the way, and enjoyed the cool feel of air coming from the fan.

She strummed her fingers thoughtfully against the small tiles. Using the Internet on her cell phone, she began shopping for a new kitchen window and floor tiles. As she did so, she moved closer to the fan, enjoying the strong breeze. *I never dreamed I could survive without central air.*

She had become so accustomed to her way of life, she'd never really considered other ways to make do. Going without air was a hardship. But not really a big one. And to her surprise, she rather enjoyed the country smells. Between the fan and breeze coming in through the screen, she was comfortable enough.

It didn't take long to find the tile she wanted. She'd show it to Eli and ask him how many to order, or if he knew of a place where she could get a better price. In the meantime, she could organize the glasses and plates that had been taken out of the cabinets and put them in boxes she'd found in one of the closets. She carefully wrapped each dish in a paper towel before placing it in the boxes.

A couple of hours later, the boxes were full. And she was thirsty, so she grabbed her tea and took a seat at the table. As she drank Lipton, she imagined what Old Sam had looked like. *I would give anything for a photo. I wonder if I inherited any of his physical traits. Or if my father had.*

She chuckled. *I already think of him as Old Sam, just like Eli does. I feel like I've known my great-uncle forever.* Of course, that hadn't been difficult. After all, the dear man had left her this beautiful property and home. But more importantly, from Eli she knew of his kind heart and his talent.

Jessica teared up. Taking a deep breath, she forced composure. It wasn't her fault that they'd never met, was it? Her parents had rarely mentioned him, and when they had, there hadn't been any hint about what a very dear person he was. Now they were gone because of a car accident.

Surely, they'd known that he was a special individual. *Is he really in heaven? Is there a God? When I asked Eli how he knew God existed, he didn't say anything to convince me to believe* .

All the same, Eli's confident declaration that there is a God had prompted her to think more seriously about eternity. An excited shiver darted up her spine and landed in her shoulders.

As she sat at the table, the theory of eternity wouldn't leave her alone. The concept had been on her mind since Eli had claimed that Sam was in heaven.

The mere thought of living on after death seemed too big to be real, but something about it was comforting to her. It felt right. She migrated to the brown sofa that directly faced the fan, and began to dust around it. The breeze swept her hair behind her ears. It was a typical hot June afternoon. Temperature-wise, Illinois was pretty much like Missouri.

She continued to assess what improvements would be necessary. Her thoughts drifted again to Eli Miller. To her dismay, her heart skipped a beat. She quickly reasoned that her reaction to him was due to her chaotic emotions.

No doubt about it, she needed Eli. Not only for fix-ups, but to learn about her uncle. By the sound of it, no one had been closer to Old Sam than the Miller family. And she'd absorb every detail about Old Sam.

But there was more to it than that, she admitted as she crunched on an ice cube. She couldn't pinpoint what it was, but something inside of her had immediately bonded to the good-looking builder. The more she considered his thoughtfulness and gentleness, the way he saw things in the most logical manner, she acknowledged that her connection to him could never be broken. He'd made her feel welcome. And what was she doing to repay him? *I'm going to sell the place that's so dear to his family.* She closed her eyes to calm herself.

My insecurities are at work. He must understand my point of view, even if he doesn't agree. Plus, I need his help. Maybe that's why I'm reacting to him with so much emotion. Because I depend on him for the improvements. More importantly, even, to learn about Old Sam. Eli is my connection to my family.

She stepped to the kitchen to refill her empty glass. As soon as she poured more tea, she began shopping for windows on her cell phone. When ugly incidents from her past began to enter her mind, she quickly blocked them out. With lots of practice, she'd learned to do it. But her efforts weren't always successful.

As she forced composure . . . again, she pressed her palms against the countertop and looked out the window. She immediately calmed when she saw her great-uncle's buggy.

There wasn't a reason to keep it, of course. But before she sold it, she'd like to take a ride in the simple mode of transportation.

For a blissful moment, she imagined Old Sam and Esther riding together into town. Another lone tear slipped down her cheek. She wondered how they'd survived a ride in the winter without heat. She imagined Old Sam helping his beloved wife in and out of the buggy. The two holding hands as they walked into church.

She smiled at the thought. She wanted a man who was a good listener. Someone who cherished her. It was something she'd never experienced. Of course, she couldn't be sure that she ever would. But she still hoped.

Old Sam must have been lonely without Esther—and his four sons, who'd died before his wife. The attorney who'd phoned her and told her about the will had briefed her on her uncle's background.

Their marriage must have been something like one would read about in a fairy tale. If Esther had been half as wonderful as her husband, they must have been the happiest couple in the world.

As she scrolled her cell phone, looking at window after window, she thought of how early death had claimed many members of the Beachy family. She pressed her hand over her heart and drew in a deep breath. She looked up at the austere walls. No pictures. *Interesting people.*

She continued through the hundreds of pictures on her

cell phone and wondered which window would look best in the kitchen. Her thoughts kept turning to her great-uncle. She'd always believed that a person's home told a lot about them. What this home revealed about Old Sam and Esther was that they had diligently adhered to the Plain Faith.

She put away her phone and made her way into the library, to the left of her bedroom. Inside the room lined with wall-to-wall shelves, she pulled out a hardcover on woodworking, then returned it to its place.

When a bead of sweat dripped down her cheek, she pivoted toward the living room to retrieve the fan. Back in the library, she set it in front of the office chair and flipped it back on.

She sat down and smiled at the large number of books. She checked their titles.

Woodworking. The Facts on Farming. Gardening. Even a book on horses and their diets. Lots of religious covers. She wasn't surprised to find a Bible on the small table in the corner.

Without thinking, she reached for it and flipped it open to where a cloth bookmark had been placed. Perhaps Old Sam had put the marker here for a reason. Maybe he'd just stuck it in randomly without thinking. There was no way to know.

The small print that said *John* at the top piqued her curiosity. *For God so loved the world, that He gave His only begotten Son, that whosoever believeth in Him should not perish, but have everlasting life.*

Jessica paused, her hand not leaving the page. It felt a bit odd to be looking at God's Holy Word. She knew people who went to church, but they'd never discussed their beliefs with her.

In fact, Eli was the only person who'd ever mentioned eternal life to her. For some reason, she'd never pursued information on Christianity, and why people believed in an afterlife.

Still holding the worn book on her lap, she looked around, digesting what she'd just read. She saw numerous Christian magazines stacked neatly, and she realized how very deeply religious Sam must have been.

Her heart warmed a moment, and she closed her eyes to savor the sweet sensation. Already, she loved him. She was certain. A strong force inside of her accelerated until she was certain she must learn everything about the hope-chest maker.

She stood and ran her finger over the dustless shelf. Either Old Sam had kept his home clean or church women had kept the place tidy while he'd been ill.

Curiosity took over, and she began to open desk drawer after drawer, searching for things that might reveal more about her great-uncle. There were odds and ends. Receipts for stain, oats and barley, groceries, mulch, plants. Some loose coins. As she held the receipts, one dropped to the floor. The fan blew it underneath the base of the bookshelves.

She got on her hands and knees to retrieve it. As she stuck her fingers under the bottom shelf, her finger touched something round. Like a button. Suddenly, her finger slid into a hole, and a small flap released.

As it did so, an envelope dropped to the floor. She stopped and pressed her lips together in surprise. She retrieved the envelope, but before looking at the contents, she reached back underneath and closed the flap. And stopped.

It's a secret drawer. As reality set in, she considered what she'd just discovered. *Old Sam hid something.*

She eyed the envelope. It wasn't flat. Something inside made a small lump.

She tried to open the envelope as neatly as she could. It was habit. With great care, she pulled both sides open and glimpsed a key. She studied it and held it close to her face. Her jaw dropped because the key wasn't a normal key, like for a house or car.

On the contrary, the key's shiny gold surface and ornate details reminded her of a pirate movie she'd once seen. The key in the movie had opened a treasure chest.

Her heart pumped to an excited beat. But what did this key unlock? She pulled the envelope all the way open. *There's more.* Careful not to tear the thin paper inside, she pulled it out and admired the beautiful print. Her gaze quickly drifted to the bottom where Old Sam had signed, *My Love Forever, Sam.*

Salty moisture stung Jessica's eyes, and she blinked. Emotion tugged at her insides while she reclaimed her chair, keeping the note in front of her. While her fingers shook with excitement, she read it out loud:

> *To my true love:*
>   *I've made you something from my heart*
>   *It's hidden in a special place*
>   *My Love, we'll never part*
>   *Our anniversary of sixty years*
>   *To find it, here's a start*
>   *It's at the spot*
>   *We both agreed*
>   *To spend our lives as one*
>   *Here and in eternity*
>   *When time on earth is done.*

Jessica swallowed a huge knot that blocked her throat. As she stared at the impeccable print in front of her, her pulse picked up.

She traced a finger over the love letter that had obviously been authored by Old Sam to Esther for their sixtieth anniversary. But she'd passed before that day. That meant that her great-uncle had hidden a gift for her before she'd died.

Of course, how did Jessica know for certain that he'd actually done so? She studied the key. And the note. Finally, her instincts told her that he had indeed hidden a special gift for Esther. Where they'd agreed to marry. *How romantic.*

Jessica stood. Without a doubt, she had to find the gift. Her curiosity wouldn't let her forget about it. Here, in the place where she'd thought she'd be bored out of her mind, she'd found something that piqued her curiosity like nothing else ever had.

Her heart pounded as she reread the letter. Afterwards, she checked it again and frowned. There was no clue where their special place was. She sighed.

Obviously, Esther never had the chance to lay eyes on the special gift he'd made her. Jessica straightened, and her mind kicked into high gear. What was the present? And where was it?

The following morning, Eli arched a brow. Jessica was acting . . . distracted. Like something was on her mind. He and Chuck worked to remove the small tiles on the kitchen countertop. Wayne was putting finishing touches on the new construction a few miles away.

While Eli cracked the dark mortar, Chuck bent to

press his hand against his right hip. My back's actin' up again. Mind if I take a break?"

Eli shook his head as he put down his tool and nodded. "*Gut* idea. Time for a drink of water."

The moment the driver stepped outside, Jessica appeared. "How about an iced tea?" Before Eli could say yes, she lowered her voice. "There's something I want to talk to you about."

"Tea sounds good." He stepped to the hall bathroom and washed his hands. When he returned to the kitchen, she handed him a full glass and smiled.

"What is it?"

She motioned with her hand while she stepped into the library. Curiosity prompted him to follow.

Eli had always loved Old Sam's library. It was common knowledge that Sam was well-read. That he couldn't start the day without reading the newspaper. And that he was always up-to-date on the weather forecast. Farmers constantly asked for his thoughts on their crops.

Eli took in the book-filled shelves on the walls. He could hear the voice of the local news announcer coming from Chuck's portable radio in the pickup.

He turned to Jessica and eyed her with curiosity.

In silence, she retrieved something from one of the shelves and carefully handed it to him. As he took the ornate-looking key, he pressed his lips together thoughtfully.

He looked at Jessica. "And? You want me to do something with this?"

As he looked into her deep green eyes, he noted a determination he'd never seen before.

Jessica motioned to the empty chair, and he shook his head. "No thanks. I'd rather stand."

Jessica reached for a piece of paper next to the books. "Here. Read this."

Raising an inquisitive brow, he took the paper from her, careful not to tear it. While he read the love letter Old Sam had written Esther, he teared up. Jessica finally stepped around him to claim the empty chair.

In silence, he held the letter closer and reread the touching words. When his gaze drifted from the neat print to Jessica's face, his lips parted in surprise.

In silence, he studied her, and his throat constricted with emotion. The compassionate expression on her face pulled at his heartstrings until he swallowed and raised his chin.

She got up from her chair. "Old Sam made something special for Esther and hid it in hopes of giving it to her at their special place on their sixtieth wedding anniversary."

He took another glance at the note before meeting her gaze. "Where did you find this?"

He watched while she sqatted down at the base of the cabinets. She pressed something, and pulled out a drawer.

Eli's jaw dropped in surprise. In all the years he'd known Old Sam, he'd never been aware that the hope-chest maker had a secret hiding place. Of course, it was most likely that no one had known. Until now.

When he regarded Jessica, he could tell that she awaited his response.

"It's a secret drawer."

"I see that." After a slight hesitation, he added, "So this is where you found the key and the letter?"

Still in a squatting position, she looked up and nodded. "I discovered the drawer by accident." She stood and planted her hands on her hips. "Eli, I've been dying to talk to you about this."

"How long have you known?"

"Not long. Where was their favorite place?"

The last statement prompted Eli to think hard. The eager expression on Jessica's face told him that she couldn't wait to see what the key unlocked. And the last thing he wanted to do was disappoint her.

His thoughts drifted back to conversations he'd had with Old Sam about his marriage to Esther. He knew so many things. Old Sam's favorite dish. That Jessica's great-uncle didn't like beets. Even what treats Esther had fed their horses.

Where was it?

A combination of excitement and great inquisitiveness edged Jessica's voice when she finally broke the silence. "Eli? Where was their favorite place?"

He chuckled. He wasn't sure why he laughed. Perhaps it was a disappointed reaction because he didn't know the answer to her question. Finally, he shrugged. "Jessica, I'm sorry. I don't have the faintest idea."

"No, Eli. Don't say that." She looked disappointed.

"But it's true."

"You said you talked to my great-uncle often."

"*Jah.* Of course. But he didn't share where he and Esther had agreed to start a life together." He threw his hands up in the air. "To be honest, this letter comes as a surprise to me."

"That Old Sam was a romantic?"

Eli could feel the pink flooding his cheeks. He wasn't sure why this discussion made him uncomfortable.

Jessica placed a stubborn hand on her hip and challenged Eli. "What's wrong with being a romantic?"

This conversation was becoming ridiculous. Where was Chuck? Why didn't he interrupt them?

She continued to look at Eli expectantly.

Finally, he gave a conciliatory shake of his head and met her gaze. "Okay. I might as well address this issue and get it over with. I just don't see Old Sam as a romantic." He lifted his palms in a casual gesture. "Maybe he was. Maybe he wasn't. At this point, it really doesn't matter."

She raised her voice a notch and squared her shoulders. "Of course it matters. You've read the letter yourself. What would you call someone, then, who so loves their spouse that they go about making something very special for an anniversary and hide it?"

Eli considered Jessica's logic. The woman had a point. The letter itself showed a side of Old Sam that Eli had never seen. Of course, Eli hadn't been around when Esther was alive. Old Sam hadn't shown his affectionate side as a husband with his beloved wife gone.

When he finally looked back at Jessica, she arched an eyebrow. "That my great-uncle was a romantic makes me love him even more. In fact, just knowing the gift he made her is hidden somewhere makes me feel compelled to find it." She hesitated as if searching for the right words.

When she continued, a combination of determination and sincerity edged her voice. "I don't know why . . ." She rolled her shoulders. "You know the story you told me about the dots? About them all being connected?"

He contemplated her question, and waited for her to explain what she was getting at.

She breathed in before continuing in a lowered voice. "Don't you see? I feel like I'm in the picture now, with

Old Sam and Esther. I don't know why, but when I go to sleep at night, I can't put them out of my mind. Now I'm not just a lone dot, I guess. In my mind, I'm on the page with all the other dots, including Old Sam and Esther. And Eli, there must be someone who knows where Sam's and Esther's favorite place was. Maybe your mother?"

Eli drew a breath and offered a conciliatory shrug. "I'll ask her. And . . . about being a romantic? I never said anything was wrong with it. In fact . . ."

"What?" Her voice had softened.

"I guess I've never thought of Old Sam in that way."

"As a husband?"

"I always thought of him as a husband to Esther. But I never knew he did things like write poetry and hide gifts."

"Eli, I'm curious . . ."

"There's more?"

She laughed. "If you were married, would you write a poem for your wife?"

He cleared his throat and said firmly, "You're really putting me on the spot, here, aren't you?"

"I don't mean to. It's just that . . . what Old Sam did for Esther . . ." She drew her arms over her chest and closed her eyes a moment. When she opened them, she slowly dropped her hands to her sides. "It's my dream. To have someone who loves me so much that they would do something with so much love. It's so sweet. And now that I'm privy to this, I feel like I have a much better picture of my great-uncle. Before, I'd respected him as a person. As someone with special creative talents. But now, I can glimpse his heart."

"To be honest, I'm still a bit stunned by the poem."

"But there's nothing wrong with that."

Eli lifted a dismissive hand. "Of course not. It's just that now, I realize how truly close he was to Esther. And that he must have missed her terribly."

"Would you ever write your wife an anniversary poem?" she asked again.

A chuckle left his throat, and he lifted his palms in defeat. "Jessica . . . no."

"Why not?"

"Well, because, one: I'm not married. And secondly, I don't write poems. So there. You've got your answer. And it's a no."

Her expression stopped him, and he found his words. "Maybe I'm just not the romantic type. I don't know. You're asking me questions I'm not equipped to answer."

"Eli, you know what I think?"

He frowned. "I'm not sure I want to know."

She smiled. "You said yourself that you're the chivalrous type."

"I did, didn't I?"

"Uh-huh."

"But that doesn't mean I'm into poetry."

With a small laugh, she said, "You don't have to be."

He watched as the corners of her lips curved into what appeared to be a combination of determination and amusement.

"But there is something I want you to do."

"You mean besides fix your kitchen? And read Old Sam's love letters?" He glanced at the desk and the clock that made an even ticking sound. "Which reminds me . . . I have work to do." He winked.

"Eli, you've got to help me find what this key unlocks. Please."

"Okay. But how can I help if I don't know where their special place is?"

Jessica snapped her fingers and smiled. "I have an idea." Before he could say anything, she went on in an excited tone. "Pretend you're Old Sam."

He lifted a doubtful brow.

"Humor me, Eli. You've lived near Pebble Creek your entire life. If you were Old Sam, where would your favorite spot be?"

He drummed his fingers against the desk and considered her question. "It would have to be somewhere where he could hide the gift."

"Right."

"Maybe in the barn?"

Jessica frowned. "Really?"

"You asked me to guess. But remember, the barn sparked Sam's creativity. And it was where Maemm, Rebecca, and Rachel used to sit and talk with him."

"You've got a point. But I just can't picture Sam asking Esther to marry him in the barn. Wherever it is, it would have to be inside. Maybe it's hidden on the back patio that faces Pebble Creek?"

He threw up his hands in defeat. "I'll let you figure this one out. Guessing their favorite place is like finding a needle in a haystack. You know how large Pebble Creek is."

"Yes, but we don't have many options. Because, like you said, wherever it is, there has to be a spot for the gift."

He grinned. "But it's not up to me to do this. I'm only half."

She lifted a curious brow.

"Because I'm pretending to be Sam, remember?"

She returned his grin.

"Let's go with you pretending to be Esther. Where would a woman's favorite spot be at Pebble Creek?"

Chapter Five

That afternoon, at Old Sam's flower bed, Jessica was more determined than ever to find what the key opened and what Old Sam had made for Esther for their sixtieth wedding anniversary.

As she took in the black-eyed Susans and coneflowers, she frowned. *You need water. Now.* As she removed the garden hose from its hook on the foundation and turned the spigot, she could hear Eli talk with Wayne and Chuck while the threesome finished the countertop.

A buzzing overhead prompted her to look for the source. She frowned at the family of wasps around a roof corner. She continued away from the buzzing insects and considered how to get rid of them. She wasn't sure. But she would find out.

She was sure that Eli would know, and she considered asking him. The last thing she wanted was to bug her handsome carpenter about everything; he was already working so hard on her house. Maybe she could just ask him who to hire to take care of the problem.

The hose slipped from her grip, and water hit the

kitchen window. She saw Chuck jump at the sound of the spray against the glass.

"Sorry!" She hollered so they could hear her. At the same time, she offered a friendly, apologetic wave. But as she focused back on what she was doing, she realized something very interesting. In fact, the more she contemplated what was happening, the tighter she gripped the hose.

The truth was, she currently worried about things she'd never even thought of in the city! And to her astonishment, she'd begun focusing more on how to get rid of wasps, eternal life, and the unusual-looking key and what it unlocked, and less about the sale of this home and her stressful drive to work. And surprisingly, in the process, she'd become much more relaxed than she'd ever been. As a pleasant result, the ugliness of her past seemed far, far away.

A clicking sound prompted her to look at the door where Eli stepped outside, holding a screwdriver.

He eyed her with amusement. "Miss Beachy, I can see I'll have to be wary of you as long as you've got that in your hand." He motioned to the hose.

As she turned to water the base of a coneflower, a fly buzzed in front of her nose, and she started to swat it away. A strong yet gentle hand came down on hers.

"Easy does it. I didn't bring a change of clothes. Speaking of which, there's a rod in the bedroom closet to hang your clothes on."

"Thanks. And sorry." She looked down.

He chuckled. "You can't blame me for being wary with that"—he pointed to the hose—"in your hand."

He lowered his gaze to her fingers.

A few steps took him to the spigot, where he turned off the water.

"There. Now I don't have to worry. Besides, a rainstorm's supposed to hit tonight." He glanced at the flowers. "They'll have more than enough water."

As she looked at him, she wasn't sure what to say. She found herself lost in the soft gray flecks that danced in his eyes. She wanted to break the deep connection she felt with him at that moment, but to her dismay, she couldn't look away. What was odd was that he didn't, either. Instead, they continued to lock gazes until she forgot the hose was in her hand and let it drop.

For a moment, she lost her voice. She was fully aware that her chest rose and fell more quickly than usual, but she couldn't slow her breathing.

He obviously didn't trust her with the hose, but she didn't trust herself when he was so close. Finally, he looked away when the buzzing started up again. They looked up at where wasps swirled around a nest.

She looked at Eli. "The last thing I wanted to do was to burden you with something else, but are they difficult to get rid of? There must be something to spray on that?"

"*Jah*. Kerosene will make fast work of them. But in the meantime . . ."

Without saying anything, he pointed to the water. "I suggest that you stay away from that. That hose in your hand scares me, and if water hits the nest, you could be in big trouble."

She eyed him in amusement. "I guess I've given you reason to be concerned."

He winked at her.

They glanced at the flower bed. After a lengthy, thoughtful silence, he resumed their conversation. "It was always important to Sam to keep Esther's flowers alive. On Esther's birthdays, after she passed on, he added flowers in her memory."

"Really?"

Eli nodded.

His gaze drifted to the plant that struggled. He shook his head and said gently, "After her death, Old Sam continued to work on this beautiful flower bed." Eli let out an emotional breath. "This was Sam's favorite."

She frowned. "The dead one?"

Eli nodded and offered a gentle lift of his shoulders. "*Jah*."

Jessica considered what Eli had just said and lifted a curious brow.

Eli nodded. "Such a shame. It looks like it's a gonner."

Jessica bent to touch the stem between two thorns. "So this little guy was my great-uncle's favorite?"

Eli nodded. "I guess it just finally gave up." He turned toward the barn.

She quickly stepped behind him. "What are you doing?"

"I'm going to grab a shovel and dig it up. No use keeping a dead plant."

She stopped and hugged her hands to her hips. "No!"

He pivoted to face her. "What?"

"We can't give up on it."

A stunned expression crossed his face as he looked at her to continue.

"Eli, don't you see?" Before he could respond, she went on. "If this was Old Sam's favorite"—she extended her arms to the garden—"I won't get rid of it until I've done everything I can to save it."

He waved a defeated hand and frowned. "But it's dead."

She lifted her chin in determination. "Maybe not."

Eli chuckled.

"What's so funny?"

"I didn't know you had a heart for green things."

She smiled. "I always root for the underdog."

A few seconds later, he nodded approval. "There's nothing wrong with that. How 'bout we leave the little guy alone for now? But I'll still check for kerosene."

A light click prompted them to turn to the door where Chuck stepped out. The driver rubbed his back and eyed some of the refinished cabinets to be installed. "Mr. Conrad sure did a fine job on these. If I didn't know better, I'd think they were brand-spankin'-new. Why, it's gonna be a different-looking room when we're all finished."

As Eli and Chuck stepped to the pickup, Jessica followed. Eli turned to her and waved. She repeated the gesture.

As she listened to the tailgate slam shut and the click of the door handles that followed, Jessica's mind returned to Old Sam's key and the gift he'd made Esther. *I have to find it.*

As soon as they left, Jessica made her way into town for cleaning supplies and food. It was good to get out of the house. Tomorrow, she'd get to see the new cabinets back in place.

Given the condition of her home and the cleanup she tried to keep up with, she wore jeans, T-shirt, and tennis shoes. She'd weeded the flower bed. Jessica rolled her shoulders and admitted that what she had on was way more comfortable than her usual attire.

She rolled down her front windows to enjoy the country smells. Since coming to the Midwest, she'd realized that sometimes she enjoyed the natural feel of the outside air more than the cold air conditioning.

She took in the fields on both sides. The horse-drawn operation still intrigued her. She pulled over and stopped the car long enough to eye the unique picture through the photo lens on her phone and clicked a picture. She took a backup image before checking her mirror for traffic and pulling back onto the blacktop.

The corn was almost knee-high. *Corn and beans. That's what they grow here.* She was fully aware that her friends from St. Louis wouldn't believe how the Amish farmed.

As she slowed the car and looked around, she couldn't rid the key and the note from her thoughts. The more she contemplated Old Sam and Esther and their undying love for each other, the more determined she became to see what he'd made her. Without a doubt, whatever it was, it would be wonderful; Jessica was certain.

Two things had become crystal clear to her since she'd moved to Arthur: One, Old Sam had done everything to perfection. Secondly, his love for Esther was the type of love that Jessica had read about in romance novels. A solid relationship that could never have been broken.

In fact, their love had been stronger than any couple's she'd ever known. Deciding she'd better pay attention to the road, she stopped at the first sign as she came into town, and considered where to park. While she did so, she admitted that the scene around her was much more interesting than what she'd normally see in the city.

She glimpsed the queue of horses tied at the Welcome Center. Empty buggies. People entering and exiting the one-story building with flyers in their hands. A parking lot full of cars.

Pedestrians walked the sidewalks. In her rearview mirror, she noticed a horse and buggy coming her way. She looked again in the mirror for a second take. Amusement lifted the corners of her lips.

She was fully aware that the simple mode of transportation wasn't rocket science. Still, it definitely piqued her interest. She wasn't sure why she was so fascinated. What she was certain of, though, was that she couldn't wait to ride in a horse-drawn buggy.

Here, there weren't crowds of people. It was much quieter. She arched a thoughtful brow as she acknowledged that this way of life wasn't all bad.

In fact, she liked it. There. She'd admitted it. She'd only been here a short time, but already there was more to spark her interest here than in St. Louis. At the top of the list was the key and Old Sam's love note to his wife. Eternal life. Buggies. Horses.

She drew in an appreciative breath. There was one more thing, or person, rather, that attracted her interest. Eli Miller. Her pulse sped up. He was so good-looking. She even liked the light scar near his right ear.

But most of all, she loved his protective nature. The way she knew she was safe when she was with him. And she wasn't sure why, but she respected his steadfast faith, even though she didn't have it.

All her life, she'd sought security. Strangely, she'd never felt it until now. It didn't make sense; she wasn't even home, in familiar surroundings. And she barely knew Eli. *How can I be so comfortable when I'm in an unfamiliar place?*

She recalled the warmth of Eli's touch on her shoulder when the slamming barn door had frightened her. She closed her eyes a moment in bliss. The she opened them. And frowned.

Stop. Don't even go there. He wouldn't even think of dating you. You're as different as day and night. He drives a buggy; you own a car. You're a city girl. He's a country boy. Besides, soon you'll be going home. And there's no way he'll be moving to the city in the near future. Or ever.

A certain conversation swept through her thoughts to make her fully realize their differences. *Besides, he believes in God. You've never even been inside of a church.*

As she took in the scene in front of her, she relaxed. A few women wore long dresses and coverings on their hair. There were regular folks, too. Like her. People sporting jeans, T-shirts, and tennis shoes.

She'd learned from Sandy that Arthur was a combination of Amish, Mennonites, and regular folks like her. And despite their different faiths, they combined to make one friendly, happy town.

Arthur was considered a tourist attraction. Brochures in the Welcome Center attracted spectators to everything Amish, from custom-made cabinets to real Amish dining.

St. Louis was a mélange of different races, backgrounds, and languages. But unlike this little town, not everyone got along. And some areas were safer than others.

Most people she knew and worked with were like her, just average folk who followed the rules. But unfortunately, the city also had its share of crime. As a precautionary measure, she carried mace in her handbag. Her apartment wasn't in the safest area. But she was there because of finances.

But not for long. She smiled at the thought of moving across town. Then she'd be safer. And closer to work. That reality prompted her to relax, and she pulled her key from the ignition. She glanced in the mirror to make sure her eyeliner was even. Satisfied, she stepped out and closed her door.

Inside the local store, two Amish girls smiled at her, so she politely introduced herself.

They did the same. Afterwards, Hannah and Miriam looked at each other with shy expressions and giggled. The young girls both wore *kapps* on their heads. Their faces were void of makeup, even lipstick. And aprons covered their long dresses. Everything about their appearance seemed so . . . innocent. Coming from a troubled family, that was something she'd never felt.

Jessica pulled her purse strap over her shoulder and began to enjoy the surroundings. The air smelled of spices. As she proceeded slowly down the first aisle, she checked out the herbs in baggies with their contents typed on a white label. Egg noodles had labels that said they were handmade by the Amish.

A circular platter displayed bite-sized pieces of cheese, and she sampled one, nodding satisfaction. Several steps behind her, a mother scolded her child for touching an item.

As Jessica proceeded down another aisle, a woman with a wide smile, also with a head covering, a long dress with an apron, and sturdy black shoes, met her gaze and stopped. Jessica couldn't help but smile back. She didn't mean to stare, but the eyes looked familiar.

The lady stepped closer and their gazes locked as she spoke with a soft voice edged with curiosity and excitement. She asked, "Jessica Beachy?"

As Jessica nodded, the woman continued with enthusiasm. "I didn't mean to eavesdrop, but I heard you introduce yourself."

She extended her hand in a friendly gesture. "I'm Annie Miller. As a very close friend of your late uncle's, I want to extend my warmest welcome." She swallowed and continued in a more serious tone, "And also my sympathies for your loss. I'm so sorry."

Jessica slowly released the warm fingers. "Thank you, Annie." Before continuing, Jessica paused. "I thought I recognized those eyes. You're Eli's and Wayne's mother?"

Annie responded with a nod and a huge smile. "*Jah.* I have another son, John, too. He's a welder. People tell me the boys resemble me. Fortunately, they're much taller!"

Annie clasped Jessica's hands in hers and pressed firmly. "I'm glad to meet you, Jessica. I can't even begin to tell you how much we loved Old Sam . . . We were so close, and he did so much for us."

Annie closed her eyes a moment as if gathering her strength. When she opened them, her eyes sparkled with moisture. Because of the woman's obvious love for Jessica's great-uncle, Jessica immediately bonded with her.

"He was dear to my heart. And I'm sure you've got a lot to do right now. But know this. I'm here for you. Whatever you need."

Jessica considered the generous offer. Right now, what she really needed was to find out what Old Sam had made Esther for their sixtieth wedding anniversary. And where he'd hidden it. As she started to speak, she caught herself and stopped the words that were about to leave her mouth. Although Annie Miller was obviously very easy to talk to, they'd just met. But maybe after some time, she could broach the subject of the gift and where Old Sam and Esther had agreed to spend the rest of their lives together. It wasn't the right time to ask.

"I'm just a call away, and I do mean that sincerely. We've got a phone in our barn, and we check messages often."

Jessica smiled and said sincerely, "I'm so appreciative, Annie."

Annie winked. "We're already friends."

Jessica nodded in agreement. After a slight pause, she went on. "We're practically neighbors. Actually, we're the first house south of yours."

Annie's grin widened. "Eli told me. I'm so glad you're close by. I'll bring you an official welcome batch of my sponge cakes. And don't forget"—she paused to put a hand on her hip—"you're welcome anytime. Old Sam would want me to make you feel at home, and that's exactly what I intend to do. In fact, Jessica, if you don't have plans for Saturday dinner, we'd love to have you. Will you come?"

That evening, Jessica unloaded the last of her supplies and food that she'd purchased in town. With the kitchen under construction, she decided to keep her new items on the table. It was as good a place as any. It would be nice having dinner with the Millers tomorrow. But tonight, there was supposed to be a bad storm.

As she organized the table, her thoughts turned to

Annie Miller, and she smiled. Eli's mother seemed so easy to talk to and understanding.

So much that Jessica had wanted to ask Annie about Old Sam's and Esther's favorite place, to tell her all about the key and the note. But talking about Old Sam should occur in a quiet place. Where appropriate attention could be given to the wise hope-chest maker.

But that didn't mean that Jessica couldn't search for Old Sam's gift. *It has to be somewhere.* She leaned forward on the countertop and acknowledged that there was enough daylight left to search the very place that had inspired Old Sam to create his works of art.

I'm ready to look.

In the old barn, Jessica eyed the ladder hanging on the wall. Then she turned to look up at the hayloft, let out a determined breath, and crossed her arms over her chest. *Eli said there's a large window at the top that overlooks Pebble Creek. Old Sam's and Esther's favorite spot could be up there. If that's the case, I could find the gift he made for her today.*

As she stepped toward the hayloft, a squirrel scurried in front of her and came to her tennis shoes, where he sat on his hind legs and looked up at her.

She laughed. "I know I've got big shoes to fill, but I wouldn't be a relative of Old Sam's if I didn't take care of you." Quick steps took her to the side wall, where she unfolded the bag of pecans.

Taking a handful, she closed the top of the container. As she began to return to where the animal had begged, she looked down and stopped.

"You followed me. Okay, I know you were Old Sam's pet, but I still don't want you to bite me, so I'll put these snacks down here."

She took a couple of steps back and placed the pecans a few feet away from the animal. She was fully aware that in St. Louis, this squirrel's life would be in danger. Here, he might be looked at as a friendly creature, but she knew people who trapped them and killed them because the long-tailed mammals were considered pests.

When the brown-furred creature scurried away through the large open doors, Jessica proceeded back to the wall and stepped to the ladder, placing one hand over one long board and the other underneath. Pressing her lips together, she leaned forward and lifted the ladder enough to remove it from its hooks.

Gripping the ladder, she carefully stepped back so it wouldn't hit her feet when she laid it down on the floor. After dusting off her hands, she gripped it again and pulled it to the front of the hayloft, where she lifted it and rested it against the edge of the loft.

Making sure the legs of the ladder were planted firmly against the cement and checking to ensure that it was steady and balanced, she glanced up. For a moment, she closed her eyes, pressed her lips together in a determined line, and forced herself to go on.

She'd never liked heights, and this loft wasn't an exception, but the drive to find her great-uncle's gift prompted her to continue her mission.

With great care, she planted her right tennis shoe on the bottom rung, careful to keep her feet in the middle, and started up the steps. On the third step, she stopped. When she was satisfied that it was safe, she continued the climb with slow, steady motions. She was glad she'd changed to jeans and a T-shirt.

She didn't look down. As she neared the top, she blinked at the bright light streaming in through a window.

For a moment, she stopped at the sting of tears in her eyes. Letting out a breath, she looked up, careful to keep balanced. *I'm almost there.*

As she reached for a support beam that extended down from the vaulted ceiling, a cracking sound made her startle. The ladder moved, and she gripped the beam and used her knee to push herself forward onto the floor of the loft.

But before she was able to get her entire body up, the ladder gave way beneath her. The sound of the heavy ladder hitting the cement prompted realization that she was lucky she hadn't gone down with it.

But she wasn't entirely safe yet. She leaned forward, moving as much of her body onto the floor of the loft as she could. Her heart thumped against her chest in urgency and fright. Hay stuck to her arms and to her hands. By this time, she'd managed to slide most of her body onto the level floorboards while her feet and lower legs dangled in the air.

You can do it.

As she struggled to swing the remainder of her body to safety, she accidentally looked down. Her pulse zoomed into high gear. She gritted her teeth so hard, she accidentally bit her tongue.

Her lungs pumped hard for air. Finally, she managed to move her feet onto the loft. Heaving a sigh of relief, she rolled onto her back and closed her eyes. When she opened them, she turned to face Pebble Creek.

As she looked out the large window, the pace of her heart started to calm. She drew in a deep breath and let it out, realizing again how fortunate it was that she hadn't gone down with the ladder.

Brushing hay off her face and neck, she recalled her

purpose, and smiled a little as she continued to gaze at the beautiful creek and the out-of-place hill.

As she turned to the hay stacked neatly in rows, she glimpsed a cabinet at the end of the bales. She straightened and observed the drawer handles with great hope and great nervousness.

But she quickly returned her attention to the window and the fairy-tale-like view. An emotional knot in her throat almost choked her. She swallowed it while tears of amazement blurred her vision.

She'd never seen Pebble Creek from this angle. She couldn't look away as she imagined Levi and Annie Miller falling in love as they tossed pebbles into the creek to see who could make the bigger splash.

She realized that she, too, was mesmerized by Pebble Creek. She broke the happy reverie when she stepped to the cabinet and began pulling the drawers open.

The view of the property is gorgeous from this window. This loft could have easily been their favorite spot. Bending, she squinted, shuffling the contents. But to her dismay, she didn't spot anything that closely resembled a gift. Frowning, she revisited the drawers, beginning at the top.

Finally, she stopped, crossed her arms over her chest, and shoved out a defeated sigh. Her gaze swept the floor and the broken ladder and landed on her cell phone, which she'd put down on the cement.

She looked around for another means to get down. She checked her watch. Unfortunately, Eli and Wayne wouldn't return till tomorrow afternoon. And she couldn't call for help, either.

After trying to come up with options, she bit her lip and frowned. There were none.

* * *

That evening, in the Millers' barn, Eli could hear footsteps outside of the entrance. He peeked out the door.

"Daed?"

His father joined him. "The clouds are coming in." As he laid a bucket next to the wall, he went on. "They're callin' for a thunderstorm tonight. Let's make sure everything's closed up good."

In silence they went about their jobs. All the while, Eli's mind was on Jessica and how to make her believe in God. The more he toyed with ideas, the more uncertain he became.

He didn't even hear his father when he joined him in the horse stalls. Levi snapped his fingers, and Eli looked up. "I finally got your attention." The stern look on his father's face stopped Eli.

"What's goin' on? You're caught up in what to do about Old Sam's great-niece?"

Not wanting to discuss what bothered him, Eli pretended a sudden interest in the pile of dirty straw. He looked down at his work and responded with disinterest as he continued raking. How was it that his father knew something was wrong?

"Ah, come on. I can read you like a book. Did you know that whenever you're worried about something, you got this crease that appears on your forehead?"

Eli smiled a little, running a finger over his brows. "I wasn't aware of that."

"No use trying to hide something. And I'm guessin' you're preoccupied with Jessica Beachy and how to save her."

Eli considered the issue and gave a firm nod. "*Jah.*

Of course I am. But we've already talked about it. And you told me you weren't sure what to do."

"I said to pray."

Eli offered a slight lift of his shoulders. "I'm definitely doing that." He breathed in and forced a smile. "To be honest, I'm realistic. I know we can't live without problems. It's just the way it is. But Daed, this trumps anything I've ever had to deal with. And I don't know what to do next."

Eli turned his attention back to the pile of dirty straw. When his *daed* didn't leave, Eli looked. "I'm glad you're here for me. Thanks for trying to help."

Eli wanted to drop the subject. But the elder Miller didn't let that happen. Instead, he nudged Eli's shoulder and motioned to the nearest bale of straw. Before Eli could get a word in, his father said, "What's the worst that could happen? That I can't help, right?"

Eli considered the logical question and offered a gentle shrug.

"Aww, come on, Sohn. Now you got me worrying about you. Let's get this out in the open."

They both sat on the bale. Eli contemplated how to broach what was on his mind. His father was right. What was the harm in talking about it? A conversation wasn't going to hurt.

"Daed, she's only gonna be here a couple more weeks. Until we finish Sam's house. I feel like God has put her here with me for a reason. But how can I make her believe? I mean, when you think about it, belief has a lot to do with faith. It's not like I can personally introduce her to the Creator of the universe and watch them shake hands."

Eli pushed out a sigh and crossed his arms over his

waist. Why were they talking about this again? They'd already been through it once. And his own father didn't even know what to do.

When his father didn't respond, Eli lowered his voice to a more serious tone. "See?" He rolled his eyes. "We didn't come up with a solution before, and unfortunately, this time's no different."

The senior Miller finally responded with a firm shake of his head. When he turned to Eli, his eyes reflected both sadness and hopefulness. "I've been praying about this. And the more I think about it, the more it's hard to believe a relative of someone so strong in their faith, like Sam, doesn't believe."

"But Daed, you've got to remember: she never met him." Eli gave a gentle shrug. "When I think back on the conversation with her in the barn, I'm glad I said what I did. That Sam's in heaven. Maybe she'll think on that. Who knows?" After a slight hesitation, he went on. "The problem was when she asked me how I knew."

"And?"

"I wasn't sure what to say. If she's looking for tangible proof, I don't have it." He gave a helpless lift of his palms and frowned. "I know I should've said something, but the question took me off guard. I've never witnessed to anyone. Now it's my mission to make sure that she knows the Lord. For her sake and for Old Sam's. But how do I do it?"

When his *daed* glanced at him in silence, he said, "There's one thing for sure, that my window of opportunity to do something important is short."

As they sat in silence, Eli couldn't help but consider the complexity of eternal life. It was something he'd always believed. But when it came right down to it, he'd never questioned it.

"This is by far the most important challenge I've ever faced, Daed. I was wondering . . ."

Levi looked at him to continue.

"Have you ever told anyone about our Savior? Tried to convince them He's real?" After a slight pause, Eli went on. "We go to church. We pray. But really . . . we haven't done what's most important, and that's to tell others."

Levi Miller let out a low whistle. "You're right, Sohn. Unfortunately, I have to say no to that question." The only sounds were from the pigeons perched on the windowsill and a squirrel that scurried behind them.

When Levi spoke again, he gestured with his hands. "Here's what I think, for all that it's worth. It's our responsibility to make sure she knows that we believe in God and why we do. Tell her the Easter story. About the stone. That Jesus's body was no longer in the tomb. That they found it empty."

He paused to adjust his hips on the bale. "As far as making her believe it really happened?" He shook his head slowly. "Sohn, that's something that only God can do. You can't expect to convince her of what she has to decide on her own."

He looked off in the distance before lowering his voice. "Believing is a choice. To us, there's never been any doubt. It's important that what you say comes out in the right way. The last thing you want to do is to shove Christianity down her throat. That could turn her off. At the same time, this is something we can't ignore."

"When did you know, Daed?"

"What? That I believe?"

Eli nodded.

The expression on his father's face reflected deep concentration. His lips were pressed together. Tiny wrinkles outlined the corners of his eyes. His jaw was set.

"I'm not sure that there was a special moment. I just always did. But you've got to admit that we're fortunate. The two of us, we were raised in Christian homes, and that's a great blessing." Eli's father bent to stare down at the floor.

When he sat up, he glanced at Eli before proceeding to stand. As he looked down, he squared his shoulders, as if a sudden confidence swept through him. "Sohn, this is something you can't do alone."

Before Eli could question the statement, his father had his hands on his hips. "Give this one to God." After a long pause, he added, "And I hope you got everything bundled up at the Beachy place. The storm's comin'."

Chapter Six

Less than an hour later, Eli contemplated the conversation he'd just had with his father. The sunset colors of orange, red, and pink filled the western sky as Eli tied Storm to a post near Jessica's house.

Flame was pulling the other buggy. After talking with his *daed*, Eli had remembered covering the open space where the window had been taken out in the kitchen. But was the space sealed enough so that the rain wouldn't get in?

A downpour was expected, and he didn't want to risk water getting into the kitchen. Thunder crackled. The air smelled of rain.

As he knocked on Jessica's door, he tapped the toe of his boot impatiently against the cement. Sliding his hands into his trousers pockets, he hooked his thumbs over the tops.

When no one answered, he glanced around the corner to confirm her car was in the drive. It was. He knocked again. This time, he accompanied the knock with a friendly holler. "Jessica! It's Eli. Are you in there?"

I'm glad we took care of the oak. Now I don't have to

worry about it falling on the roof. A bolt of lightning flashed, reminding him of the urgency to check the plastic. Besides, getting home by horse and buggy would be much easier while the weather was still dry. He turned the handle and cracked the door. "Jessica!"

Inside, he breathed in the pleasant scent of vanilla. He noticed an unlit candle on the small table next to the couch. A plastic glass was next to it. The windows were still open. Obviously, Jessica wasn't inside. But why hadn't she closed the windows? Surely she knew a rainstorm was coming.

Quick steps took him to the kitchen, where he checked the plastic covering on the inside of the window. Satisfied, he went out to make sure the exterior of the window was sealed as well.

He nodded satisfaction. Rain wouldn't get in. Then he remembered the open window in the living room. He didn't like being in Jessica's home when she wasn't there, but he figured what needed to be done couldn't wait.

Outside, the temperature dropped a few more notches while the wind picked up speed. Eli turned at the loud whinny where Storm stomped his foot impatiently. Grinning, Eli made his way to the beautiful animal and ran an affectionate hand over his long nose.

"You love rainstorms, boy. Well, you're going to have a happy night. But I want to get us out of here before the big one hits."

I can't go until I find Jessica. Where is she?

Concern prompted him to frown. He guessed that she knew the forecast, but his protective nature took over, and he couldn't leave until he saw that she was inside, safe and sound.

He walked around the house. The branches of the

large oaks were swaying. The coneflowers struggled to stay put as the wind tried to sweep them away. When it started to sprinkle, Eli stopped and looked around.

To his dismay, Old Sam's great-niece was nowhere in sight. *But her car's here.* There was only one other place to check, and that was the barn.

Noting the dark turmoil in the sky and the rain that was picking up its pace, he decided it best to take the horse with him to the old structure. Storm was a sturdy creature, for sure, but if the downpour hit, Eli wanted the animal inside where he wouldn't be hit by something the wind threw his way.

He untied Storm before leading him to the barn.

As they made their way toward the red building, Eli frowned as he recollected the conversation he'd had with her about the whereabouts of Old Sam's gift. *She's in the barn, looking for it.*

As soon as he stepped through the large doors with Storm, the suddenly fierce wind blew them shut. Storm threw his head back and let out a long whinny at the loud sound.

"Let's put you where Old Sam kept his fella."

Old Sam had never installed gas lights in the barn, and the sun was gone for the day, so the lack of light made Eli blink to adjust his vision. He could see well enough to retrieve the flashlight that Old Sam had kept next to the horse stall.

He flipped it on, led the standardbred into the stall, and aimed the beam at the soft, urgent voice.

"Eli! Over here!"

The moment Eli glimpsed Jessica standing in the hayloft, he stopped and put his hands on his hips. "What—"

He shone the light on her as her hands flew in the air. "The ladder broke."

He shone the light on her face. "I can see that."

Her voice hinted at her excitement. "I was looking for Old Sam's gift to Esther!" When he didn't respond, she went on. "Remember you told me that the window up here"—she motioned with her hand—"offered the most beautiful view of Pebble Creek?" Before he could get a word in, she continued. "You were right, Eli. I can't believe—"

Tapping the toe of his boot to an agitated beat, he cut in. "Did you find the present?"

She shook her head.

Eli dug his one hand deep into his pocket, aimed the flashlight with the other, and blew out a frustrated breath. His heart pumped too fast to be considered healthy.

Finally, he chose his words. "Jessica Beachy, what if you'd been on the ladder when it broke?" He didn't try to hide his irritation.

She stammered as branches of the nearby oaks hit the structure with ferocity. "I was . . . I had almost made it to the top when it—"

He interrupted. "Jessica, what you did . . . it was foolhardy. You were alone." He raised his voice. "Do you have any idea what could have happened to you?"

He removed his hand from his pocket and clenched it at his thigh. The more he contemplated what could have happened, the tighter he clenched. Finally, he dropped his hands to his sides and groaned. The light focused on his boots. "I'm so upset right now, I should leave you up there to teach you a lesson!"

He pretended to leave, and the heels of his boots made a light sound on the concrete . . .

"Eli! I'm sorry! I can't undo climbing up here. What happened was an accident!" The soft urgency in her voice added to his irritation. Her timbre . . . her plea that came out so sincere and raw . . . it did something to him. His emotions . . . they were a strange combination that he had never experienced. Anger, relief, and to his dismay, a strong desire to take care of Old Sam's great-niece.

He paused to consider what was tearing him up inside. He was sure that Old Sam would have expected him to protect Jessica. Without a doubt, Jessica's uncle would have counted on Eli to keep her safe.

But he admitted that his loyalty to Old Sam wasn't the only reason. And that admission flirted with his emotions until the acknowledgment bordered on anger. *What am I doing? This is an Englisch girl who lives in the city. She doesn't even know God. We're as different as night and day, so how can I feel this way?*

Confusion swept through him as he acknowledged that he *needed* to take care of her. Required it as much as the air he breathed. And he was every bit as certain that she needed him.

He aimed his flashlight up at the loft to see Jessica moving closer to the edge. She looked down at him. "I'm sorry. It never even occurred to me that the ladder would break. And . . ." She stopped to catch her breath. "I didn't get hurt. It's okay. The last thing I intended was to upset you. But please stop chastising me and get me down from here."

He ignored her plea. "You could have broken bones or worse." Lightning illuminated the loft for a brief second. The moment it struck, he glimpsed Jessica's eyes. And the turbulence in them only added fuel to the fire. He yearned to feel the softness of her honey-blond hair. To tell her everything would be okay.

Stop. He cupped his chin with his palm. After a long, thoughtful silence, he forced composure and adopted a tone that was half warning and half sympathetic. "I'll help you on one condition."

She flung her hands in the air. "What?"

"That you promise to never try anything like this again unless I'm with you."

She nodded. "I promise." As he was about to reply, she leaned forward.

He held up a hand. "Don't come any closer. There's no guard rail. I'm afraid you'll fall."

She took a step back and a newfound calmness edged her voice. "I appreciate your concern for me, Eli. But I'm not sorry I came up here."

Her comment gave him pause. He lifted a brow. "What?"

For a moment, he let the beam of light drop to his feet. But he quickly aimed it back up at the loft.

"You heard me." She turned and pointed to where the window was. "I know you can't see it from where you stand, but you told me the loft offered the most beautiful view of Pebble Creek. And you were right. I wouldn't have traded it for the world."

Suddenly, a relieved breath escaped him, and he realized that what she'd said was true. The part about her being okay, anyway. That nothing bad had happened. And of course, he was convinced that this incident would only reinforce her determination to find Old Sam's gift to Esther.

Jessica's drive to do what she wanted challenged him

in ways he'd never known. And to his surprise, she was making him take a stronger look at his faith. He was every bit as determined to protect her as she seemed determined to be independent.

He tried to imagine how badly she wanted to know the great-uncle she'd never had the pleasure of meeting. As loud thunder rumbled in the background, he realized he couldn't undo the risk Jessica had taken. And most of all, he needed to get her down. But how?

Rolling his shoulders to get rid of the knots, he said, "I'm sorry I got upset."

He turned and paced a few steps before making his way back to the front of the loft. As he looked up at her, an emotion claimed him that was so strong, he could barely get his words out. Even more confusion set in, and he tried to appear calmer.

He realized that he owed her an explanation for his anger. "Jessica, I don't want anything to happen to you."

He put one foot in front of the other and pressed his right palm against his hip as he transferred the flashlight to the other hand. "Do you understand that your uncle would have wanted me to protect you? To make sure you stayed safe?"

She nodded.

"That's exactly what I intend to do. But . . ." He stopped to chuckle. "You're certainly not making it easy."

A chill swept up Jessica's spine, and she closed her eyes at the uncomfortable sensation. The temperature had dropped several degrees since Eli had found her.

As a bolt of lightning illuminated the sky with a flash of brightness, she wrapped her arms around her body and ran her hands over her arms to warm them. A long silence passed while Jessica watched Eli search for another ladder.

At least, that's what she guessed he was trying to find. As she looked on, she swallowed, recalling the unexpected conversation that had just occurred.

She could hear the horse clomping its hooves against the floor of the barn. Every time the lightning would flash or the thunder would crackle, the animal would let out a loud whinny. But what amused her was that it seemed to enjoy the bad weather rather than fear it. Maybe it was her imagination. She wasn't sure.

But what she was certain of was the sudden, unexpected tranquility that filled her heart and soul. Being here in the storm, in a hayloft with no ladder, with Eli and his horse, raised a question.

Why does this make me happy?

After searching for answers to her question, she finally took a deep breath of relief. As Eli's footsteps went from wall to wall, she acknowledged what she already knew . . . his exceptionally strong loyalty to her beloved uncle and his desire to carry out Sam's wishes. Or what Eli believed Sam's wishes to be.

As that truth gelled inside of her, she glanced at Pebble Creek. Of course, she couldn't see it now. But she knew what it looked like by heart.

Blades of deep green grass floated with the breeze on both sides of the narrow body of water. The incline that led up the hill. The curve of the creek as it snaked its way through the land. Two-story houses that were spread out miles apart in the background.

At that moment, she acknowledged the great connection between her uncle, his property, and the Millers.

But strangely, she strongly felt she belonged in their picture of unity. She drew in a surprised breath and covered her heart with her hand. That very realization stunned her so much that she didn't hear Eli trying to get her attention.

"Jessica? You okay?"

She stiffened. "Sure. I'm fine."

But she wasn't sure if that was true. Her stunning admission that she belonged to Pebble Creek and the Miller family forced her to come to terms with many uncertainties, not to mention that she yearned for Eli to care for her because of who she was, not because Old Sam would have expected it.

But who is Jessica Beachy? She looked down and contemplated the question. And what was special about her that would cause Eli to be interested in her, even without her great-uncle's genes?

She didn't have an answer. When she returned to reality, she glimpsed Eli and wondered how long he'd been standing below the hayloft. She lifted her chin and forced a confident smile.

"No extra ladder. I'd go home and get ours, but I'd have to reach Chuck to give me a lift back here with his truck. The weather's too bad to take the buggy out."

The horse let out a loud whinny and clomped its hooves.

Eli responded with a laugh.

"He's spoiled, isn't he?"

Eli gave a slow nod. "That he is. Storm. He loves storms. We named him appropriately."

The admission prompted a grin. Jessica wondered what it would be like to own a horse of her own.

Eli rolled his eyes and focused on Jessica. "But enough

of that for now. I've got to come up with a way to get you down."

"What do you have in mind?"

He cupped his chin with his fingers and raised an undecided brow. Finally, she followed the beam of his flashlight to what appeared to be a rope.

He held it out in front of him and shone the light on it. "The only option right now is this. That is, unless you don't trust my skills."

"I trust you, Eli." She wasn't sure why she did. The floor seemed a long way down. Especially by rope.

Suddenly, she had second thoughts. "Eli, I've never even tried to climb a rope, let alone get down from . . ." She shrugged. "From anywhere. So I think the rope idea's out."

"But you said you trusted me."

"I do . . ."

"All you'll have to do is hold on to it and do as I say. If you do that, you'll be back on ground level before you know it."

She found herself agreeing. "Just tell me what to do."

"Okay, Miss Beachy. First of all"—she watched as he made some kind of knot—"I created an eye splice, and I'm going to toss this up to you."

"Okay."

The loft went dark as she heard the rope fall near her. The flashlight beam was quick to return, and she glimpsed the rope. She retrieved it. "What do you want me to do with it?"

He pointed. "You see that hook?"

She followed the flashlight. "Yes."

"Just hang the knot I made on that hook. I left enough of a hole in the middle to slip it around the metal."

She followed his instructions.

"Make sure it's in place."

She checked. "The knot goes over the hook."

"One more thing."

"What?"

"Now I'm going to toss the flashlight up to you. Shine it on the rope as I climb."

"Okay."

She caught the flashlight, aimed it on Eli, and watched as he tested the strength of the nylon. With steady motions, he pulled on it before climbing. Jessica shouldn't have been surprised at the ease with which he made his way up to the loft. As he did so, he kept one foot over the other.

When he reached her, a smile of relief tugged at the corners of her lips. "Is there anything you can't do?"

She sat on the nearest bale. Not responding, he took a seat next to her. "Let me catch my breath. Then I'll get you down."

The realization hit her that her alone time with this handsome Amish man was coming to an end. That thought wiped away the happiness she'd just experienced at the prospect of getting down.

She enjoyed this time with Eli. In fact, she could spend all day in his company. He protected her. And even though he did it for Old Sam, he kept her safe. Still, she wished with all her heart that Eli acted out of his interest in her, and not because of her great-uncle.

She turned to him. As she did so, her hand brushed his with affection. He quickly pulled it away. She realized that all Eli would ever be to her was a happy dream. Something she wanted but would never have.

"Ready to go down?"

Her jaw dropped. "Yes, but . . ."

"What?"

"I'm having second thoughts."

She acknowledged that she'd been so happy being with Eli, she'd neglected to realize that she'd have to make it to ground level. That the ladder was still broken.

She straightened and forced her attention on what needed to be done. "I'm going to need your help."

"Getting down is pretty easy, actually. It's all about technique."

She lifted an inquisitive brow and listened.

"Just remember this. Hand over hand, and lean back until you're in a sitting position. The correct hand placement will protect you from rope burn."

"That's all I have to do?"

"*Jah.*" He lifted his palms. "That's it."

A bolt of lightning made a loud crack, and she jumped. He reacted by taking her by the arm. Knowing that all she was to him was Old Sam's niece, she gently pulled away. Although she enjoyed his reassuring touch, she didn't want to lead herself on.

The flashlight was between them, so she wasn't able to see the reaction in his eyes. Finally admitting that she had no choice, she nodded. "I'll try."

Eli got up, and she followed him to where the rope was hooked. Nervousness edged her voice, and her hands shook. "Could you show me what to do so I can imitate you?"

"Sure. First of all, I've got to figure out where to place the flashlight." All she could think about was how she was going to make it down the rope. What if she lost her grip?

"Okay." It took a few moments to decide where to put the flashlight. Finally, he placed it between two rafters so that there was a good view of the rope leading down to the cement.

"I'll show you how easy it is."

Without responding, she watched as he grabbed the rope with one hand and put his free hand over it. He spaced his feet against the rope and leaned back. In a few seconds, he'd made it all the way down.

He climbed back up to her. "Are you ready?"

Too nervous to find her voice, she nodded.

"Okay. I'll go first, and you'll be right above me. And don't worry. This rope's not going anywhere. Remember, I'm beneath you and I won't let you fall. But don't let go of the rope. If you can at least hold on, I'll get you down."

She swallowed. "Okay."

"Ready?"

She nodded. He started down. "Come on. Hold on while you wrap your feet around the rope."

The moment she did what he suggested, she nearly lost her grip. As she slid downward, she landed midair on his body.

"It's okay, Jessica. I've got you. Just hold tight to the rope. Hand over hand as we work down."

As he supported her body, she held on to the nylon. Inch by inch, she went with him. To her surprise, she didn't fear falling. She knew Eli wouldn't let her. But what she feared was how comfortable she felt this close to him. Like he protected her. The warmth of his body and his woodsy scent made her close her eyes a moment. At the bottom, he steadied her from falling.

When they locked gazes, he let go of her and smiled a little. "Mission accomplished, Miss Beachy. As soon as the rain lets up, I'll get you back inside the house." A long silence passed until he broke it. "You're safe and sound."

As the rain hit the roof, she said seriously, "Eli?"

He looked at her.

"Thank you."

He responded by dipping his head.

"While we're avoiding the storm, I was wondering if . . ."

"What?"

"Would you tell me more about God? If He's there, I want to know Him."

Saturday morning, Eli extended his arm and tossed the fishing line into the deep lake behind the Conrad home as he considered his serious conversation with God the night before. *Did I say the right things to Jessica?*

He furrowed his brows while a cool breeze caressed his forehead as the sun began to show more orange.

To his right was his brown tackle box. On the ground to his left was a bottle of water. In front of him, two dragonflies circled each other. In the background, oak branches moved with the warm breeze. There was an occasional croak of a bullfrog.

His gaze on the water, Eli saw a fish jump, then splash back into the lake.

"Now that's a big one!" his *daed* commented. Eli didn't respond.

The last thing he wanted to do was strike up a conversation. They were here to fish. He was sure that voices hinted to the fish that they'd better skedaddle.

When Eli fished, he preferred to focus totally on just that. Unfortunately, his father and best friend must have come to socialize.

His father's voice encouraged him. "He's teasing you, Sohn. He knows you're on a roll and he's determined to not let you catch him. I don't know what you're using for bait, but whatever it is, the fish are goin' wild for it."

Eli nodded.

On his opposite side, William Conrad's son, Jonah, chided, "You must be in just the right spot. At this rate, you'll have enough bass to feed every family in town."

Eli lifted a doubtful brow. "Not if the fish know we're here."

Several heartbeats later, his *daed* cleared his throat. "Someone takes this a little seriously, I'd say."

Jonah added, "That probably explains why he's catchin' all the fish."

Eli tried to humor the two. He didn't want to make this a social hour. At the same time, he wanted plenty of fish tonight for the Millers' and Conrads' yearly outdoor fry.

After taking a swig of water, he glanced at Jonah. "It's a good day," Eli agreed. "But I'm goin' for the record."

"You mean from last year?" Jonah inquired.

"Mm-hmm."

Eli's father chimed in. "Between the four of us, we caught over thirty bass and croppie. 'Course, William was here with us."

"I wish Daed could have come," Jonah added.

"We probably set him behind schedule with the Beachy cabinets."

When the two companions regarded him with curiosity, he explained, "He knew we were rushed for Jessica's cabinets. And he was kind enough to move us to the front of his queue."

"And that's what friends are for," Jonah said in a confident tone.

"Hopefully, he'll be able to relax this evening and enjoy our efforts."

"*Jah,*" the oldest son of William and Rebecca agreed. "I can already taste the first bite. It's going to be some dinner."

To Eli's chagrin, the conversation continued. *And they wonder why they haven't caught anything.*

"There's not a woman in the good old US of A who wouldn't die for the batter our mothers came up with together."

The statement prompted Eli to recall a recent conversation with Maemm. Still eyeing his line, he spoke in a barely audible voice. "The fish have migrated to another part of the lake."

Jonah ignored the statement. "It was when they were at Old Sam's. When they were kids. Annie was eating sponge cakes with Sam while Maemm worked next to her on a dried floral arrangement."

When Levi's line moved a little, Jonah stopped talking. But some time later, the movement proved to be a false lead.

Jonah chugged some water from his Arrowhead bottle before screwing the top back on and placing it next to his tackle box.

To Eli's chagrin, he went on. "From what I recall about the conversation, my mother said that Old Sam was reminiscing about the days when Esther used to make her grandmother's recipe for fish batter. He insisted that no one could ever match the taste of the secret recipe."

Jonah pulled in his line to re-bait the hook. With one fluid motion, he positioned the reel behind his back and flung the line into the water.

"Good toss," Levi commented. "You've got yourself quite an arm. So did they ever find the recipe?"

Jonah shook his head. "No. And they never will."

Eli and his father glanced at him to go on.

"It was a family secret. In fact, it may not have even been in writing. But"— Jonah chuckled—"You thought that was the end, didn't you?"

Eli rolled his shoulders and smiled a little. "Obviously, it's not. Go on."

"When our mothers were canning tomatoes together, they tried to replicate Esther's recipe. Maemm had been in Esther's kitchen when she measured ingredients for the fish batter."

Eli cut in. "So she remembered what was in it?"

Jonah nodded. "Some of it. But after Esther went to the Lord, Maemm and Annie tried on numerous occasions to combine their memories to recreate Esther's special batter. And what they came up with might not be identical, but it's got to be the best I've ever tasted."

Eli lifted a brow. "Of course, no one cooked like Esther. At least, that's what I'm told. Too bad she didn't let anyone in on her secret."

Jonah agreed. "*Jah*. Because she surely wouldn't have wanted Old Sam to be without her good meals."

"It just goes to show you that life's short, and we can never take anything for granted. Especially a great fish batter."

Eli considered the statements and swallowed an emotional knot. Life was short. And that made it even more important that Jessica know the Lord before she returned to Missouri. He couldn't bear the thought of her not becoming a Christian. He grimaced.

Long moments passed while the three remained silent. It had become obvious to Eli that he hadn't had as much as a bite since this talk had started. Even though he enjoyed chatting with his best friend and his *daed*, common sense told him it was time to relocate.

He reeled in his bait. As he did so, his father and Jonah directed their gazes to the line.

"Hey, watcha doin'?"

Eli caught the line with his hand and grinned. "I'm going to find where the fish went."

"But we've got to catch up."

"'Bout what?" Eli responded, gathering his gear.

Jonah chuckled. "About how the Beachy house is coming along. I helped on the cabinets. Did his niece like our work?"

Eli didn't respond as he watched Jonah's line move. Something toyed with the bait. Eli stood very still until he realized that whatever had teased Jonah's bait had left.

"Hey, why don't you ask Old Sam's niece to join us tonight."

Eli smiled a little and nodded. "Maemm already did."

Eli would never forget when they'd met. She'd been wearing a dress and high heels. At his new spot, he set up his pole and tossed his line again. It hadn't taken long for her to convert to blue jeans, T-shirts, and tennis shoes. He couldn't help but wonder if she'd found time for the crosswords she'd brought with her.

And at first, she hadn't displayed an interest in the outdoors. Now, she was attempting to nurse a dying rosebush back to health. She'd really taken an interest in the Amish and in learning what she could about her great-uncle. Not to mention that her vivacity captivated him. She made him feel special. Needed. All of that was fine. The problem was, he liked her. A lot.

To his dismay, he was growing attached to a girl who was way out of bounds, not only because of her lack of faith, but also because soon, she'd be gone.

It was obvious that he had to stymie his interest in her. And right away.

"Earth to Eli." His father's voice interrupted.

"Daed?"

Levi rolled his eyes. When he spoke, his voice hinted at combination of amusement and frustration. "Don't take it so seriously, Sohn. You're focusing way too much on the fish and too little on the camaraderie."

Levi lifted an inquisitive, challenging brow. "That's what's going on here, right?"

Eli gave a half nod, knowing he avoided the truth because there was no way he was going to admit to his best friend and his father that he harbored a romantic interest in Jessica Beachy. It would cause great concern in their community. And talk.

He drew in a low breath at what he'd just admitted to himself. That he was enamored of Old Sam's great-niece. A woman who would be leaving the state in just a few weeks.

At that moment, Jonah shouted in excitement. "Got one!"

Eli and his father immediately rested their poles on their respective spots and stood on either side of Jonah, who was reeling in what appeared to be the biggest bass that Eli had ever seen.

"You've got 'im!" Eli said in a combination of encouragement and excitement.

"Easy does it!" Daed's voice continued to coach Jonah as he reeled in the catch. When the struggling fish was within reach, Eli and his father helped Jonah remove the hook from the large mouth and toss the flopping fish into the styrofoam container with the other fish.

"It's your turn next, Daed!"

That evening, Eli's mother embraced Jessica before motioning to the others in the room. "*Willkommen!* Jessica, meet William Conrad."

A tall man with a light brown beard stepped toward them, extending his hand in a warm greeting. Jessica shook his rough, callused hand, quickly noting his broad shoulders.

A couple tiny freckles on his face gave him a youthful appearance. But despite his long sleeves and his broad-fall pants, it was hard not to notice his muscular arms that tried to push out of his shirt.

She took advantage of the opportunity to thank him for redoing her cabinets. "They're absolutely gorgeous! Of course, they'll look even better when they're installed and off of the floor! When I planned how I wanted them to look, never in my wildest dreams did I expect such ornate detail."

He dipped his head. "We do our best. So glad they meet with your approval."

Still conscious of the eyes on her, she went on. "Not only that, but you put me at the head of the queue, and I'm so appreciative."

He smiled. "It's the least I could do for Sam's kin." His eyes moistened. Jessica's heart warmed. She felt a bond with the owner of Conrad Cabinets.

"Old Sam was like part of our family. I can't count the number of times he came to our aid. And helping you is a small way to thank him for bringing so much to our lives."

Softly, she said, "Thank you for that, William."

He glanced down at the floor before meeting her gaze again.

The woman with a pretty face stepped up to speak. She had a creamy complexion and chestnut-brown hair that was tucked up neatly under a white *kapp*.

"When I was young, and even after I married William"— she waved a hand at the handsome cabinet maker and smiled—"there were times when things happened in my life, and I didn't know what to do. Like when we went to Indiana to help William's father." She wagged a dismissive hand. "That's a story for another day." Jessica noted that William lifted a brow while he smiled in amusement. "But Old Sam . . ." She closed her eyes for a moment and gave a gentle lift of her shoulders. "He always steered me in the right direction. In fact, he played a large role in how William and I ended up together."

"Really?"

She nodded. "And your great-uncle was so wise: He must have known every proverb in the book. And he could always fix whatever was wrong."

She stopped and grinned. "By the way, in case you haven't guessed, I'm Rebecca Conrad." She laughed. "Sorry for the delayed introduction." She extended her hand in a kind greeting. "It's so nice to meet you."

"I call her my better half," William interjected with a chuckle.

Rebecca's fingers were warm when Jessica shook them. When their gazes locked, she took in the woman's flawless complexion. But to Jessica, her most striking feature was her generous smile. Jessica didn't know William and Rebecca yet, but without a doubt, they loved each other. She could tell by the way they looked at each other.

Rebecca pointed to the door. "Our clan's outside; they're anxious to meet you!"

Jessica followed Rebecca out the back door, where the delicious scent of grilled fish made Jessica's stomach growl. It was then that she realized she'd skipped lunch.

After Jessica met their five boys, a young girl, who looked to be sixteen or seventeen, joined her mother, fondly taking Rebecca's arm in hers and leaning toward her with affection.

"This is my only daughter, Mary."

The girl lowered her lashes in shyness, but when the corners of her lips finally curved upward, her contagious smile immediately warmed Jessica's heart. Mary shoved a loose strand of hair back under her *kapp* and adjusted her thick glasses before shaking hands.

"Rebecca! I need you in the kitchen!"

Rebecca squared her shoulders and lifted a hand in farewell.

"Duty calls!"

Jessica was left alone with Mary. She smiled at the girl, wondering what to ask an Amish teenager.

"How's the flower bed doing at Old Sam's?"

Mary's softly asked question surprised Jessica as she took in the girl's serious expression. Light brown hair was neatly tucked under her *kapp*, and tiny freckles spotted her rosy cheeks. Because of the thick lenses, Jessica wasn't able to glimpse her eye color.

Surprised that Mary knew about the beautiful garden,

Jessica smiled a little. "The coneflowers are doing well. So are the black-eyed Susans."

"How about Sam's special rose?"

The question gave Jessica pause. "You know about it?"

Mary offered a big nod. "'Course. Maemm and I were good friends with your uncle." She lifted a curious brow and looked Jessica in the eyes. "Did you know that my mother even used Old Sam's barn to dry flowers?"

At that moment, Jessica recalled that Rebecca was one of the three who'd taken Old Sam under their wings after Esther had passed, and Rebecca had been the girl who'd picked him fresh flowers.

She took a deeper interest in what Mary had to say. "Yes! I'm glad you reminded me. Since I've been here, Mary, I've learned a lot at once, and now I'm starting to sift through everything."

Mary beamed. "Of course. I'm actually a lot like my mother, you know. She has her own floral business; her specialty, really, is weddings that the Englisch have. The Amish aren't as much into flowers, I guess. Anyway, I help her; in fact, Maemm has a special garden for plants she uses just for arrangements. And right now, she's letting me work with her on an upcoming wedding. And some day, Jessica . . ." She closed her eyes and breathed in. Then she opened her eyes and smiled with excitement. "I'd love to have my own home and a large garden just like hers!"

Jessica's heart warmed at her enthusiasm. Jessica had just met her, but already, Mary's excitement for plants was obvious.

"I'm sure your mother's happy that you take an interest in what she does."

Mary offered an eager nod. "*Jah*." Then she said in a confidential tone, "You wanna know a secret?"

Jessica replied with a quick nod.

"Someday, I'd like to have a greenhouse."

"What a nice dream!"

Jessica considered the dying rosebush and suddenly realized that Mary was the obvious person to go to for help.

"Mary, you've got a green thumb. And I'm really concerned that Esther's special rosebush won't make it."

Mary pressed her pointer finger against her chin. When her glasses slipped down her nose, she quickly pushed them back up. She frowned. "What's wrong?"

Jessica explained the state of the plant. After she'd finished, she shrugged. "I don't want to lose it, but so far, it's just not responding to my TLC."

"Sounds like Old Sam's rose needs more than TLC, Jessica. What it needs is doctoring."

The more Mary talked about the plant, the more she amused and intrigued Jessica. She wasn't sure what the majority of Amish girls talked about, but she suspected it wasn't plants.

Finally, Jessica gestured with her palms up. "What should I do?"

Mary pressed her lips together thoughtfully. "I can think of several things to remedy this dilemma. For starters, you want to cut off the dead cones before they begin infecting the healthy ones."

"Okay." Jessica continued to listen with interest.

As they talked, they started making their way to where Levi and Eli were grilling fish. Focused on her conversation with Mary, Jessica lifted her hand in a wave to the men, and they waved back.

"And of course, a little mulch around the base of the plant will help to keep moisture in. Think of it as a blanket that keeps a baby warm."

Jessica nodded in understanding, still amused and impressed by the advanced maturity level of this young girl. If she couldn't see Mary in person, she would have believed she was talking to an adult.

"That sounds like good advice. But I think it's in dire need of something stronger. In fact, the window of opportunity to revive it may already be over. Is there a quick fix? I don't expect miracles overnight, but is there something we can do to expedite its recovery?"

Jessica waited while Mary stared at her black shoes. When she finally met Jessica's gaze, she snapped her fingers as if she'd just figured out what to do.

"Hmm. Sounds like it's time for me to give it my special medicine."

Jessica lifted a surprised brow. "Medicine?"

"*Jah.*" Mary grinned. "That's what I call it. I've experimented with my own roses, and I've come up with a combination of bone meal, blood meal, fish meal, Epsom salts, and a few other ingredients to do resuscitations."

Jessica smiled at the girl's mannerisms.

"That's never let me down. If you like, Jessica, I can take a look at the bush myself, and do what I can to save it." She paused. Seriousness edged her voice when she continued. "Did you know that was the last rose Old Sam planted in memory of Esther?"

Jessica's jaw dropped.

Mary nodded. "And that's why we've got to keep it alive. It would have been important to Old Sam. Don't worry, Jessica. I'll fix Esther's rose." She followed with a confident lift of her chin. "But you need to help."

"How?"

"Pray."

When the families gathered around the picnic tables and lawn chairs, Levi raised his voice. "Hey, everyone! We're blessed to be here together. Let's bow our heads and thank the good Lord for our blessings."

Jessica did like the others. As she listened to Levi bless the food and ask help to serve God, Jessica wondered how a God, if indeed there was one, could even hear a prayer. Especially with all of the other prayers that must occur at the same time. The thought was mind-boggling.

"And we thank You, Lord, for bringing Jessica to us. If she still wants to sell once her place is fixed up, please bring a nice family to Old Sam's. A family to make new memories at Pebble Creek. And will You please bless Old Sam's great-niece with love, joy, and true happiness that can only come from You. Amen."

A unanimous "Amen" followed.

Annie nudged Jessica to start the food line.

"Oh, I can't!"

"*Jah*. You must. We're celebrating that you're here. When God takes something from us, he always gives back something in return. He's taken Old Sam, but he's given you to us."

Slightly embarrassed, Jessica started the line. She considered Annie's theory and felt slightly ashamed. Because it wasn't quite true. Yes, Old Sam was gone. But Jessica wasn't here for good. And she couldn't hold a candle to her great-uncle.

In a voice that was heard above the talk and laughter, Annie said, "You've got to try out my fresh creamed peas. Straight from the garden. So are the strawberries and asparagus. There won't be much more till next year."

At the outdoor table, Mary made herself comfortable on Jessica's left. Annie sat on her right, and the other adults sat at her table with the kids filling up the other one and the lawn chairs.

As Jessica tasted the fresh peas, she closed her eyes in delight and swallowed. "These are the most delicious vegetables I've ever tasted!"

On the opposite side, Levi smiled. "I would say thank you, but God gets the credit."

As friendly chatter picked up volume and ice cubes clinked against glasses, Jessica contemplated this outing, and as she absorbed the kindness, she realized something that surprised her. She was more at ease with these gentle people than she was with her coworkers.

In her entire life, she'd never been this happy. While she plucked a bright red strawberry and put it into her mouth, Levi's prayer replayed in her mind. *If Jessica still wants to sell when the place is fixed up, please bring a nice family to Old Sam's. To make new memories at Pebble Creek. Please bless Old Sam's great-niece with love, joy, and true happiness that can only come from You.*

Chapter Seven

Monday, on the way home, Eli fastened his seat belt while Chuck pulled away from Old Sam's home.

"That kitchen sure is comin' along just fine. In fact, it looks so good, it could be on the cover of one of them home magazines."

"It's one of our best projects," Eli agreed.

As Eli rolled his window down, the driver's cell phone beeped. "Chuck here."

As he conversed with his wife, Eli considered everything on his plate. He let out a sigh. Before meeting Jessica Beachy, his life had been simple.

Now, his head swam with things he'd never given much thought to: How to make someone believe in God. Pebble Creek going up for sale and who would live here. Even the gift that Jessica was so determined to find and the possibility that Old Sam had been a romantic.

As the driver continued discussing where he and his wife could find the best deal on a new washer and dryer, Eli lowered his gaze to the pop can that he held with one hand on his right thigh. *Jessica not knowing the Creator of the universe is by far the biggest issue I've ever come across. But there's something else that's weighing me down. I have feelings for Old Sam's niece. She's not only non-Amish, but she doesn't even know the Lord. Not to mention that she's going to leave in two or three weeks. And I want her to stay. But if she would decide to stay, then what?*

Eli recalled that Doc Zimmerman hadn't been Amish before marrying his wife, Rachel. And Eli's own father had been Englisch before joining the Amish church with Maemm. But why were his feelings for Jessica more of an issue than his *daed*'s or Doc Zimmerman's? *No, they weren't Amish, but they'd believed in God. And they lived here, not out-of-state.*

Eli attempted to prioritize every issue that flitted through his mind. But right now, there was too much chaos going on inside of him. He pulled in a deep, determined breath and crossed his legs. What could he do?

Then the answer came. The moment it did, he closed his eyes and smiled as a feeling of both guilt and relief swept up his arms and settled in his shoulders. But he didn't try to rid himself of the sensation. Because it consoled him.

Finally, he was fully aware of how to manage his struggles. His entire body relaxed. The nervous, quick pace of his heart slowed.

The tenseness in the back of his neck evaporated. The pain in his chest went away. Maybe Jessica didn't know God. But Eli was acting like he didn't, either. A huge sense of shame overtook him, and he lowered his gaze to his boots.

How could he have forgotten that God guided his life? His Heavenly Father was in charge of everything. These issues were more difficult than others in his past, but in the entire scheme of things, with God in charge, how could Eli make the wrong choices? He had forgotten that his Savior was stronger than any problem.

He bowed his head. *Dear God, please help me to do Your will. You know my heart. My feelings for Jessica Beachy. Please fill her heart with Your love so that she may know You and serve You. And please let the unspoken bond we feel for each other be focused on You. Please guide me. Amen.*

In Jessica's kitchen the following afternoon, she glimpsed the Conrads' shiny black buggy in her drive and smiled a little. The bright sun coming in through the windows lightened the brass handles on the new cabinets a notch. As Mary prepared her special formula for Old Sam's rosebush, the fan made a light noise while the blade whirled at high speed.

Jessica sat down at the table and eyed the room with satisfaction. "So what do you think of the improvements?"

Mary glanced her way a moment before returning her attention to measure a powderlike substance and adding it to her plastic bowl. "They're marvelous. In fact, I love everything Eli has done. And the cabinets . . ."

Jessica noted a light pink that shaded the girl's already rosy cheeks.

"I love the makeover Daed did," Mary continued. "But you know the change I love most?"

"What?"

"The new window. It's so much larger than Old Sam's. And sunlight's a good thing. I always feel that it's God's way of smiling at us."

The corners of Jessica's lips curved upwards. Not

because she agreed with the Conrad girl, but because of the conviction and certainty in her voice as she'd said it. The statement had been spoken like God was her friend.

"*Fertig!*" Jessica assumed that the word meant *finished*.

Jessica rose and pushed her chair in while Mary gave her mixture a final stir.

Jessica opened the door, and the two stepped around a pile of plywood and plaster from the remodel before making their way back onto the sidewalk that led to Old Sam's flower bed.

Excitement edged Mary's voice as she bent to touch a purple coneflower. "It seems like they get more beautiful every year."

Without saying anything, Jessica motioned to the only plant that wasn't green and in bloom.

She stood next to Mary as the girl knelt for a better view of the stems. Her glasses slid down her nose a notch, and she pushed them up and pressed on the earpiece. Jessica observed her with a combination of curiosity and admiration.

Auburn wisps of hair had escaped Mary's *kapp*. It amused Jessica that the Amish called it a *kapp*, because when she heard the word *cap*, a young boy with a baseball cap immediately came to mind.

Sturdy black shoes covered Mary's feet. A white apron protected the front part of the girl's long-sleeved navy dress, which hid her legs. Jessica was sure that Mary didn't look at herself in the mirror and specifically think that she was attractive; by now, Jessica was fully aware that the Amish focused on a person's heart, not looks.

But even her long dress didn't hide curves that most

English girls would love to have. Despite the thick glasses on her face, the girl could be considered stunning. But what impressed Jessica most about Mary Conrad was her keen interest in plants and her knowledge.

Most teenagers that Jessica knew were mainly interested in cell phones, makeup, and clothes. But as far as natural beauty went, Mary had the complete package: looks, brains, and most importantly, kindness. And what made her even more special was that she didn't seem at all aware of it.

Mary made herself comfortable on the ground in front of the rosebush. Jessica sat down next to her and pulled her feet close to her body. Mary pulled clippers from her small bag, and began snipping some dead branches.

As she did so, she darted a smile at Jessica. "First, I'll prune it to get it in the best shape possible. After that, I'll feed it my special formula. I want to do everything I can so that it will absorb the vitamins and minerals."

The girl's fingers were delicate looking, and the expression on her face was a combination of thoughtfulness and enjoyment. For an odd moment, Jessica wondered what her own life would be like today had she been raised Amish.

When Mary's glasses slipped down her nose again, the girl shoved them back up. "What did you think of last night's dinner?"

"Oh! It was so much fun, Mary. The food was delicious, but you know what I enjoyed even more?"

Mary looked up before returning her attention to her task at hand. "What?"

"The camaraderie."

"I'm so glad! I'm sure you've figured out by now that we Amish folk like to get together."

"And you're good cooks, too!"

Mary lifted her shoulders in an undecided shrug. "Some of us are, and some of us aren't."

Jessica eyed the girl with speculation. "Do you like to cook, Mary?"

"Not so much. Maemm would like me to take a more serious interest in the culinary field, but to be honest . . ." She shrugged again. "I'd be telling a lie if I said I like being in the kitchen."

She laughed, and Jessica joined her.

"At least you're honest. But surely, there are worse things in life than that."

Mary shook her head as she clipped a dead rose and added it to her growing pile. "If I were Englisch, it might not be such a big deal. But when I'm an Amish *maemm*, I suppose it will matter to my house full of children."

Jessica leaned forward a bit and raised an inquisitive brow. "You plan on lots of kids?"

"*Jah*." Mary gave a big nod of her head and continued tending to the bush. "I can't wait to have little ones running barefoot in the house. To read the Bible to them at night. Say prayers with them. But Jessica . . ."

"What?"

Mary wagged a dismissive hand. "Oh, it's nothing."

"It must be something. Tell me what you were going to say. Please."

"Jessica, if I'm going to have a houseful of children, that means I'll need a husband. And"—she hesitated before continuing—"that means I'll have to find one."

Jessica laughed. "You've got plenty of time for that."

A disappointed expression crossed Mary's face, and she shrugged before returning full attention to her job.

From Mary's reaction, Jessica was sure there was more to the story than Mary had mentioned. At the same time, she didn't want to appear nosy, but she felt compelled to reassure this kindhearted girl.

"Mary, you're only sixteen."

"But other girls my age already know who they want to marry, Jessica."

Jessica considered the statement before saying gently, "And you don't?"

Mary rolled her eyes, and they lit up in excitement. "*Jah*. I know who I'd like to spend my life with."

"Then what's the problem?"

The corners of Mary's lips took a sudden drop. "I think he's got his eyes on someone else."

"Oh." Trying for something upbeat, Jessica edged her voice with enthusiasm. The last thing she wanted was to see this special girl be sad. "Things could change."

"I don't know. For some reason, no one's interested in me. I mean, not to marry."

After contemplating the statement, Jessica's words came to her, and she said with confidence, "Consider us in the same boat."

When Mary stopped what she was doing and looked up, Jessica raised her palms. "I've never had a love interest. And no one seems to be vying for my attention. Yet I'm still breathing."

"But have you wanted to get married and have a dozen kids since you were five years old?"

Jessica raised a surprised brow. "No, I can't say that I

have. In fact . . ." She wagged a dismissive hand. "Oh, never mind."

"What?"

The stressful past rushed back into Jessica's memory, and she breathed in a sad breath. "Mary, for most of my childhood, I didn't have time to think about it. So many other issues took priority."

Mary stopped her task and looked at Jessica with interest.

The last thing Jessica wanted was to dump her problems on this delightful plant-guru. So she shrugged dismissively and tried for a positive, casual tone.

"I think my past was probably much different than yours, Mary. You see . . . I didn't have time to think of marriage and kids." She swallowed an emotional knot. "My father was an alcoholic."

"Oh!"

"It's okay. Please don't worry about me. I survived. And now he's gone. So is my mother. But growing up . . . I guess you could say it was . . . tumultuous. In fact, I'm just starting to recover and get on with my life."

"I'm so sorry, Jessica. And I thought my problems were serious. I won't talk about it anymore."

"No. It's okay. I enjoy chatting with you. But excuse me for prying, and you don't have to answer this if you don't feel comfortable, but who is this boy you like?"

Mary put her weight on her other hip and lowered her voice. "It's Wayne Miller." With an innocent smile, she pressed her pointer finger against her lips and said, "Shh. This stays between us, okay?"

"Absolutely."

Jessica cupped her chin in her hand and nodded acknowledgment. "I can certainly understand why. He's a nice young man. Very responsible and hardworking."

"*Jah.* I see him at church."

"Does he know you like him?"

"I'm not sure. I mean, how would he?" She rolled her eyes. "When we're together, I never know what to say to him. Tell me, what on earth do I talk about with a boy my age?"

Jessica looked away a moment. When she returned to look at Mary, she wasn't sure what to tell her. "Let me think on that, Mary. Without a doubt, he's really into woodworking. But to be honest, I'm not sure what his hobbies are. What does he enjoy? Is there an interest you could share with him, maybe?"

"Not that I know of. Oh!" She snapped her fingers in sudden recollection. "He's really into horses."

"Is he into plants?"

"I don't think so."

"Let me ask you this, Mary. Why do you like him so much if you have nothing in common?"

Mary laughed. "I have no idea!"

Jessica laughed, too.

Mary went on. "That's not really true. I like him for what's important. It's about how he makes me feel. He's extremely thoughtful and kind. Once, when we were little, we were walking to school together on the black-top, and a car came out of nowhere and nearly hit me. He pulled me out of the way. Then he walked me to my house and told my folks what had happened. Of course, Maemm asked him to stay for dinner, and he did."

Mary put down her clippers and shifted to better face Jessica. She sneezed.

"Bless you!"

Mary pulled a tissue from her apron pocket and blew her nose, then apologized. "My allergies are at it again." But as she started to get back at her task, she stopped and smiled again at Jessica. "Do you want to hear another reason I like him?"

"Yes!"

Mary cleared her throat before continuing. "One time, when it was raining so hard after church, he held an umbrella over my head while he walked me to my buggy. I'll never forget when his shirt sleeve touched my wrist." Mary paused and drew in a dreamy breath before pushing it out. "Jessica, haven't you ever met someone like that? A person you're just drawn to? A guy you love being with because they make you feel special without even saying anything?"

Eli immediately came to Jessica's mind, and she stiffened. She strummed her fingers nervously against the concrete patio. As she did so, a fly landed on her hand, and she swatted it away. "Now that you mention it, yes."

Mary turned her attention back to the bush and snipped away. "So you understand exactly what I'm talking about." After a slight hesitation, she went on in a hushed voice. "So do you want to marry this man who makes you feel special? Do you want a family with him?"

Jessica fidgeted with her hands and pressed her lips into a straight line. Her breath rose and fell to a nervous beat. Her shoulders stiffened until a dull pain at the back of her neck prompted her to reach behind her head and rub it.

Without warning, this pleasant conversation had taken an intense turn. Jessica felt compelled to explain, but wasn't sure what to say. Because she didn't know the answer. A long silence ensued while she focused on Pebble Creek. Even from a distance, she could see the winding stream and the hill that seemed out of place.

Suddenly, the pain at the back of her neck ceased. She breathed easier, and it came to her that just the mere sight of Pebble Creek had done more to relax her than anxiety pills had ever accomplished. If only she could take this beautiful, comforting view with her.

When she realized that the Conrad girl eagerly awaited a reply, she finally decided on a response. "Mary, just because I like being around someone doesn't necessarily mean that I want to marry them."

"No?" Before Jessica could answer, Mary went on. "Does the guy you like being with enjoy being around you, too?"

Careful not to give away that the individual they discussed was someone Mary knew very well, Jessica considered the potent question. Finally, she said, "I'm not sure. I think so."

They looked at each other. As Jessica took in the curious expression on Mary's face, she considered this unusual conversation with a teenager. The girl sought advice about what she obviously considered a serious dilemma, and Jessica couldn't help her. But she wanted to. But how could she advise about something she knew nothing about? Suddenly, an idea came to her. "Mary, I know what Eli would tell you." Before Mary could question her, Jessica continued. "He'd tell you to pray to God." Jessica shrugged. "It seems to work for him."

"Eli." She shoved out a breath of relief. "He always knows just what to do. Prayer." When Jessica didn't respond, Mary asked in a more curious tone, "You pray, don't you?"

Jessica slowly shook her head.

Mary's eyes seemed to double in size. "No?"

"No."

"Why not?"

Jessica shrugged. "How do you know He exists?"

Several heartbeats passed while Mary stared at her with devastation and shock. Finally, she smiled softly and eased the tone of her voice. "I just do. Pray, Jessica. And I'll pray for you. God is with you all the time, whether you realize it or not. He brought you to us, didn't he? I consider that a tremendous blessing. When Old Sam went, I was devastated. I knew he was old, and his death at over one hundred years of age certainly wasn't a surprise; still, it was hard letting go of someone I loved so much. I can't imagine not being close to God. I depend on Him every single minute. I pray for guidance. To stay safe. And to serve Him and only Him."

When Jessica started to speak, Mary went on. "You know, sometimes we're so busy that we overlook miracles in our lives. Think about it, Jessica. Life is a miracle. Don't you ever wonder how this"—she waved a hand at the property—"all started?"

Jessica pondered the question as Mary went back to her work. But the girl's words stuck in Jessica's mind. Long moments later, Mary finally broke the silence and changed the subject.

"Jessica, I'm also going to pray for this rose, because it's special in more ways than one. Did you know that when this plant blooms, it produces a unique-looking bud?"

"Really?"

"*Jah*. It's a classic long-stemmed rose. When people talk about roses, this is what they typically think of. They're ideal for bouquets. And this one in particular is called a Bella'roma. When it blooms, it's yellow, and the tips are a reddish hue." She paused. "You know what I said about miracles?"

Jessica nodded.

"Well, this is definitely one." Her voice dropped to a tone edged with wonder. "How on earth could any plant produce such a beautiful, ornate-looking flower without a Creator?"

Jessica pressed her lips together thoughtfully. The girl made a good point. "It sounds absolutely beautiful."

"It is. That's why Old Sam liked it enough to plant it for Esther's birthday in memory of her. And oh"—Mary took an excited breath—"I wish you could smell its sweet fragrance! You'd absolutely fall in love with it, Jessica."

"I can't wait for it to revive!"

Mary darted Jessica a wink. "In my heart, I believe it will. It's special. But it's certainly not the only gorgeous plant in the world. You want to know what my favorite of all time is?"

Jessica looked at her.

"It's a beautiful hybrid tea called Chicago Peace."

"How is it different from this little guy?"

"It's got quite a history. It was bred in France in the early nineteen hundreds. Later, it was introduced in the Chicago area. It's hardy, which makes it easier to grow than some, and it's a perennial. If you're not into plants, that means that it automatically comes back every year. What's cool is that it gets pretty large for a rose."

"How big does it get?"

"About five feet."

"Wow."

"*Jah*. And it doesn't require much maintenance; of

course, it always helps to be aware of the pH and water requirements."

Jessica listened.

"It's amazing all of the different flowers that God created. And each has its own identity to make it unique." Before Jessica could absorb all that Mary had said, the girl unexpectedly jumped up from her sitting position and ran her hands over her apron. "Time for finishing touches. Just a moment . . . I'll be back."

Mary brushed her palms together. As she stepped to her buggy, Jessica got up and followed her.

Mary reached inside and pulled out a small plastic bag. "Mulch?"

"*Jah*. After I pour the mixture around the bush, I'll cover the area to help keep moisture in. That will give the rose a chance to absorb my vitamin mixture." In an optimistic gesture, she lifted her shoulders. "Then it's up to God to work His magic. Prayer."

Jessica wasn't sure how to respond.

"Because in the end, whether the rose lives or doesn't stay alive is up to God. And I'm convinced that prayers influence His decision."

As Jessica considered Mary's theory, they walked back to the roses where Mary lowered her voice to barely more than a whisper. "Old Sam knew how I loved nurturing roses. In fact, he used to tell me not to complain about the thorns, to be happy that the bush has them."

"He was so wise."

She nodded. "And you know what I liked most about him?"

"What?"

"His proverbs. There wasn't one he didn't know. And

when I worry about something, I try to think of a proverb to help me put things into perspective."

Jessica knelt on the opposite side of the rose and met the young girl's gaze before she resumed her task at hand. "What would he have said to me about selling this place?"

Mary paused and looked down at the ground. As she did so, she pressed her lips together into a firm line. When she looked up at Jessica, her lips curved into a gentle smile.

"I think I know which one he'd use. He used to say that the structure of a home isn't important. It's the people in it who count."

The following evening, Jessica watched as Eli's crew pulled out of the long drive and slowly disappeared down the blacktop. She pressed her lips together in deliberation. For several moments, she considered all that she'd put on Eli's shoulders since she'd come to the countryside.

As the warm breeze blew some strands of hair in her eyes, she carefully shoved them back over her ears and quickly decided that Eli Miller got more than he had bargained for. Not only was he fixing her house, but she was leaning on him to help her to know about her great-uncle. She was fully aware that inside, Eli still grieved. Yet she was pressing him for information.

As always, the thought of Eli prompted a smile. She breathed in and stepped away from the kitchen. As she went to the side door, she turned to take in the improvements. *This is becoming a gorgeous room. I'd love to take it back to St. Louis.*

She admired the beautiful cabinets. She carried one of the boxes of plates to the kitchen and began to unwrap them and return them to the cabinet shelves. As she moved her finger over the wood shelves, she frowned and acknowledged the need to dust first.

She found the Murphy Oil Soap and sprayed it on the lower shelves. As she ran a cloth over the beautiful wood, she breathed in the pleasant scent. She climbed up on the countertop using the step stool that Eli and Wayne had left in the room and continued to spray and wipe the top shelves.

Afterwards, she used Windex to clean the glass. Installation of the large floor tiles had begun, and already, the kitchen had taken on the rustic and modern look that she so wanted.

The fireplace bricks looked like new. When the countertops were finished and the wall opened up, the place would be fit for a magazine cover. It would be hard to leave this place.

She quickly turned her thoughts to the conversation she'd just had with Eli. His obvious lack of desire to find what Old Sam's key unlocked disappointed her.

Though, of course, why would Eli care about finding it? Even though he'd been a dear friend to her great-uncle, he wasn't Sam's own flesh and blood. And perhaps not having met Old Sam made Jessica even more determined to learn about him so she could feel part of his life.

Her cell phone rang, and she answered.

"Jessica, it's Sandy. Are you sitting down?"

Jessica fell back onto the nearest chair. "I am now. Why?"

"We have a very interested buyer."

A combination of tension and excitement made Jessica tighten her grip on the phone.

"Already? That's great! It's not even listed."

"We may not have to. A businessman from out East has gotten wind of your property. He doesn't plan to live here, but he's very interested in the Amish and is toying with the idea of purchasing Pebble Creek for a vacation home."

Jessica stiffened and absorbed what she'd just heard. Her heart pumped with excitement. And doubt. Pebble Creek meant a lot to the Miller family, and they wanted a family to buy the place and make new memories. That's what Eli's family yearned for. They strongly believed it's what her great-uncle would have wanted, too.

"Jessica? Are you still there?"

Jessica realized that her agent awaited a response. So Jessica thought of what to say. "That's good news, Sandy. I'm glad there's interest. Hopefully, it will sell quickly. I'm really hoping, though, for a family to have it. We've talked about it . . ."

"Honey, no promises, but his agent tells me that if this guy decides to make an offer, you'll be able to name your price."

After Jessica ended the call, she clicked off her phone and let out a sigh. She frowned at the news. Because if this actually materialized, the Miller family would not be happy.

The following Saturday, a light knock startled Jessica. Eli wouldn't be back till Monday. She stepped toward the entrance and checked the peephole. As soon as she opened the door, she faced a friendly smile.

"*Gut* morning, Jessica."

The woman handed her a plate.

Jessica smiled and met the woman's gaze with joy. "Thank you, Annie." Jessica held the plate closer, breathing in the light scent. "They smell delicious."

"And they're still warm. I just took them from the oven."

As Jessica eyed the fragile-looking desserts with enthusiastic curiosity, Annie laughed. "They're sponge cakes. My specialty. And your great-uncle loved them."

Jessica motioned to the table. "Please, Annie. Have a seat. I'm so glad you're here."

Annie looked around and nodded satisfaction. "Beautiful. Old Sam would approve, I'm sure."

"You really think so?"

"*Jah.*"

Jessica sat opposite Eli's mother. It wasn't hard to feel at ease with this woman because she was so friendly and because her smile was so genuine. Her hair was tucked underneath a *kapp*, and her voice was soft and kind.

Suddenly remembering her manners, Jessica pressed her palms against her thighs and lifted her chin in a newfound confidence. "Would you like a glass of sun tea? I just brewed a fresh pitcher. Nothing fancy. Just good old Lipton."

"Thank you, Jessica. That would be nice. My! The fireplace looks new!"

As Jessica stepped to the kitchen, she motioned. "I hope you'll excuse the mess."

Annie waved a dismissive hand. "Oh, that's to be expected. And trust me, I've been there. I remember when we built our home. For six months, there was only one usable room, and that was the living room. But all

the while, we imagined what it would look like in the end."
She smiled. "And believe me, it was worth the mess!"

Jessica reached for two plastic glasses. She set them
down, pulled an ice tray from the freezer, and twisted it
to release the cubes. They clinked as they fell into the
glasses.

She proceeded to pour from the gallon pitcher.

Jessica returned to the table with the two beverages.
She placed one in front of Annie and the other in front of
her chair. Then she grabbed two paper plates and two
plastic forks from a bag and winked. "To make things
easy, I'm using disposable cups and plates." Jessica
leaned forward. "I've been dying to talk to you, Annie."

"About what?"

Jessica considered the question and smiled with a
shrug. "Everything!"

The two shared a laugh.

"For starters, do you know where Old Sam's and
Esther's favorite spot was?" She continued to explain
about the letter and the key.

Annie frowned. "No, I don't. Now you've piqued my
interest."

Jessica went on. "Annie, I want to know how you and
my great-uncle became so close."

Annie breathed in and looked away before meeting
Jessica's gaze. "Where do I begin? There's so much to
tell." Annie blinked at the sting of tears. "I guess I could
fill you in on how the three of us took care of him after
Esther's death."

"You mean Rebecca, Rachel, and you?"

"*Jah.*"

Jessica took a drink.

"If I had to choose the starting place for my relationship

with your great-uncle, I guess it would be right after Esther passed on. Of course, I'm sure you already know that. When she succumbed to pneumonia, Sam went through a difficult time." She paused. "Ironically, he eventually passed from the same thing."

Jessica parted her lips in sympathy. "Poor Uncle Sam."

"*Jah.* He lost a lot of weight after Esther died. Wasn't talking much. It must have been hard." Annie took a quick drink and held the beverage in her hand. "I mean they were married nearly six decades. Jessica, I knew I had to do something. And since Esther had been famous for her sponge cakes, I thought that if I learned to make them, and feed Old Sam, then he'd cheer up." She lifted her shoulders in a light shrug.

Jessica's eyes widened. "And did he?"

"Eventually." Annie grinned. "At first, my cakes didn't turn out like Esther's. Of course, you realize that Esther was the best cook around. So I had big shoes to fill."

Jessica nodded.

"But Maemm helped me. And I kept trying." Annie's smile widened, and she lifted her chin a confident notch. "Eventually, Old Sam told me that I'd give Esther a run for her money with the desserts."

Jessica closed her eyes in delight as she took a bite of the cake. "They're delicious."

"*Denki.*" Annie nodded. After a pause to drink more tea, she went on. "I guess you could say that the rest is history. I took him sponge cakes once a week. Sometimes more." Annie lowered her voice. "I couldn't let him starve. But it's funny what happened . . ."

"What?"

"Old Sam loved to talk, so I'd stay and chat while he worked on his hope-chest lids." She drew her hands to her chest with affection. Jessica's heart melted as she realized the pain her great-uncle must have experienced and the wonderful Amish neighbors who'd done all they could to cheer him.

"Eventually, we got our Old Sam back, he gained weight, and he took to making hope chests more seriously than ever. To be honest, Jessica, I think that using his creative talents really pulled him through."

Jessica nodded her head in agreement. "And of course, he must have missed Esther's cooking in a big way. Good thing you learned how to make his favorite desserts."

Tears sparkled in Annie's eyes. "Those two . . . they were such a special pair. That's for sure."

Jessica recalled the two other girls who'd helped him and leaned forward, swirling the tea in her glass to mix with the melting ice. "How 'bout Rachel and Rebecca? What did they cook?"

Annie held up a finger while she finished a bite of the white cake. After she swallowed, she picked up the conversation. "They didn't. But they filled the void that Esther had left in other ways. Funny: God gives each of us special talents to help others."

Jessica stiffened. *God*. It slid off of Eli's mother's lips as if He were a close friend. When she mentioned Him, it was as if she knew Him. Just like she'd known Old Sam.

"Rachel always had a big heart for animals, especially horses." A fond laugh escaped Annie's throat. "That girl would sit with Sam for hours and listen to his horse-and-buggy stories, Jessica. Sam loved to reminisce. And with Rachel, he had an attentive audience, that's for sure."

"And Rebecca took him fresh flowers, right?"

Annie nodded. The pink glow in Annie's cheeks and the friendly timbre of her voice told Jessica right away that the three must be best friends. And they'd all played a role in her uncle's recovery from the loss of his dear wife.

"Ever since I've known Rebecca Sommer . . ." She rolled her eyes and corrected herself. "'Course that was a long time ago. It's Rebecca Conrad now . . . Anyways, she always had a thing for plants."

Annie grinned. "Old Sam let her dry plants in his barn, and she made arrangements at a very early age. After she married William, she actually started a business and with every arrangement, she attaches a bit of scripture." Annie lifted her palms in a gesture of amazement. "You see what I mean about God making us each with our own talents?"

Jessica didn't respond. Instead, she absorbed Annie's belief in God and contemplated her theory that He'd given everyone their own talents. She wasn't sure if God was or wasn't, but the question piqued her interest. If He did exist, what unique talent had He given her? The question pulled at her until Annie's voice broke her from her reverie.

"Jessica?"

Jessica smiled a little. "Sorry. I guess you could say that my interest is piqued. About Old Sam. And other things."

Annie slid her chair closer to the table and said in a serious tone, "You want to know something, Jessica?"

Jessica gave an eager nod while leaning forward in her seat to listen.

"You're already family to us."

Tears stung Jessica's eyes, and she blinked. Annie's voice indicated pure sincerity. A knot obstructed Jessica's throat, and she cleared it. Emotion hit her from every direction, and she considered what to say. She'd never been good at communicating her feelings; of course, her parents hadn't, either. The Miller boys and their folks had already touched her heart in ways she hadn't imagined possible. She had to show her appreciation.

"Annie, I don't know what to say." The chirping of birds on the windowsill was the only sound while Jessica tried for the right words. "Just two weeks ago, I was nervous about coming here. Uneasy about staying by myself in the country. Worried about things that needed to be done to the house and the stress of selling it. But . . ."

Before continuing, she flung her hands in the air in a helpless gesture. "You're all so very kind to me." Finally, she sat up straighter and lifted her chin a notch. "Thank you."

Annie dipped her head. "You're more than welcome. I may be partial, but I happen to believe that we Amish excel at hospitality. And . . ." Her eyes lit up and she straightened in her seat. "I just had an idea. Since you're so interested in your uncle and what he did, I'm going to show you something!"

Chapter Eight

Annie's buggy bounced a little as she and Jessica rode to the Millers'. As the horse's tail swished back and forth, Jessica breathed in the comforting scents of nature and animal.

As she adjusted her hips on the blue velvety fabric for a more comfortable position, she contemplated Old Sam's key and the letter he'd written Esther. The buggy was open, and the warm breeze caressed her face. Glimpsing Annie in her peripheral vision, she breathed in satisfaction and smiled a little.

"I love riding in the buggy."

"You didn't have to tell me."

"No?"

Annie shook her head. "I can tell by the contentment on your face. I was just thinking about how you and your great-uncle resemble each other. Did you know that Old Sam loved taking his buggy to church?" She paused. "In fact, he looked forward to it all week. Back in the day, about twenty years ago or so, he used to have a horse named Ginger and a dog named Buddy. And before that, they even had a horse called Strawberry."

Jessica turned to better face Annie. "Really?"

"*Jah.* And he spoiled them like they were his grandkids. Of course, Buddy also got a taste of my sponge cakes." She laughed. "The moment he spotted me walking toward the barn, he'd wag his tail."

After a brief silence, Annie went on. "I'm excited to show you my hope chest, Jessica. Before you leave here, you'll know Old Sam just by seeing what he did for others."

"That will be wonderful, Annie."

At the Miller home, Jessica looked on as Annie tied their horse to a post near the house.

Jessica stepped closer and offered a hand. "Can I help?"

"No, but thanks." Annie gave her a quick grin. "We Amish girls are pretty quick at this."

While they talked, Jessica began stroking the horse's nose. The horse responded by letting out a whinny.

"That means that Flame likes you."

Jessica got so close to the horse's face, their noses nearly touched. "Flame?"

Annie offered a quick nod. "It's really Wayne's horse. I don't know what it is between those two, but there's something going on."

Jessica lifted a brow.

Annie laughed. "You could say that they're bonded. Of course, Wayne takes after his *maemm*. I'm an animal lover."

After Flame was tied, Annie and Jessica followed the winding sidewalk to the house.

"I can't believe how beautiful your home is, Annie."

Annie smiled a little. "I married a builder."

* * *

Jessica loved the Miller home. She sat at the dining room table and watched Annie put some things together on the kitchen countertop. The surroundings were simple, yet Jessica didn't really feel anything was missing from the gorgeous dwelling.

With great interest, she took in the shiny hardwood floors and the sky-blue material that decorated the windows. The curtains were pulled back and attached to small hooks. Light coming in through the windows made her blink.

Of course, there were no family pictures sitting around. Eli had told her that the Amish don't believe in taking photos. All the same, hints of what the Miller family was like were evident throughout the house.

Jessica noted two different daily devotional journals. One was on a small end table to the right of the couch, and the other on a slightly larger table next to a rocking chair. An oversized bookmark stuck out from what was obviously the Holy Bible next to a devotional.

A winding circular stairway that boasted glossy oak steps wound its way up to the second story. Jessica supposed that the bedrooms were upstairs.

On the wall above the very first step was something in a frame. Curious, Jessica stepped up to what appeared to be something from Levi and Annie Miller's wedding.

As if reading her thoughts, Annie stepped closer to answer Jessica's unspoken question. "My mother and father have the same thing on their stairway wall. In fact, Maemm made that for Levi and me."

Jessica traced her finger over the embroidered date and names of Levi Miller and Annie Mast. Beautiful lilies decorated the four corners. And at the bottom, *And the greatest of these is Love*, was embroidered in a beautiful shade of blue.

Jessica swallowed an emotional knot. The words stopped her thoughts. Love. Did she have that in her life?

Jessica quickly dismissed the troubling question and focused on the cabinets. "They're cherry?"

"Uh-huh. The credit goes to William Conrad." She waved a hand. "Gorgeous, aren't they?"

Jessica nodded.

"Levi and his *daed* . . . they specialize in the actual construction of homes, but William Conrad inherited his cabinet-making skills from his own father. Unfortunately, Daniel passed away years ago, but you might be interested to know that he was Englisch."

When Jessica lifted an inquisitive brow, Annie waved a hand. "That's a story for another day, but now, let's go upstairs."

Jessica followed Eli's mother. As they made their way up the stairs, Jessica took note of the beautiful structure of the home. Cream-colored walls met extra-tall ceilings. Jessica hadn't seen the interior of any Amish homes— other than Sam's, of course—but she guessed that a lot of extra detail had gone into building this house.

Jessica paused to take in the beautiful piece at the foot of the bed. She focused on the gorgeous chest. It was smaller than what she had visualized. But the detail was exquisite. Without a doubt, her great-uncle had been a true artist. With a combination of excitement and emotion, Jessica moved closer and squinted to better view the sponge cake recipe.

As she did so, a bolt of guilt struck her, and she stiffened. She admired this kind, generous woman so much. In a way, Jessica hoped the businessman didn't make an offer on Old Sam's place. The thought of disappointing the Miller family made Jessica bite her lip.

Annie's soft, honest voice made Jessica's guilt even stronger. A pain began throbbing at the back of her neck.

"Jessica, know that you're family. I'll do whatever I can to make you feel extra welcome here. Your great-uncle was so special to me and played a huge role in my life, especially in how I view things." She added in a confidential tone, "Do you know that he even gave me advice on what to do to be with Levi?"

Jessica turned to face Annie. "Really?"

Annie nodded. "Not only was your great-uncle a great artist, but he had a heart of gold and offered great wisdom. I always thought of him as a grandfather. Of course, I can't speak for Rebecca and Rachel, but I'm pretty sure they feel the same. And even though he was much older than us, when we talked, it was as if he was on our level." She lifted her palms in a helpless gesture. "He understood everything."

As Annie watched the girl admire her great-uncle's work, her heart nearly melted. For some reason, the scene touched Annie in a way she'd never imagined. She reasoned her sentiment had to do with her love for Old Sam and that she still grieved the loss of her dear friend.

Jessica knelt in front of the chest. With a soft, uncertain voice, she looked up at Annie as she continued tracing a finger over the sponge cake recipe that was meticulously etched into the wood.

"Did you ask him to make this just for you?"

Annie gave a quick shake of her head. She pulled up the oak rocker with a blue blanket tossed on top.

"You can open it." Annie nodded toward the lid.

Jessica hesitated. "Are you sure? You must keep what's most special to you in here, Annie."

"I do, but you won't be able to see the lining if you don't look inside. Go ahead. I want you to see the pretty velvet."

Slowly, Jessica opened the lid and took a small, uncertain breath. She turned to Annie and smiled. "The lining looks like it's part of the wood. I wonder how he did this." After a thoughtful pause, Jessica's voice cracked with emotion. "He made everything to perfection, didn't he?"

Before Annie could finish her nod of agreement, Jessica went on. "Even the lining."

"But Jessica, this particular hope chest is much more to me than a work of art." She hesitated. "I keep my journal in it. I've written every night for years. In fact, I started noting my most private thoughts as soon as your uncle gave me this."

Jessica's eyes widened. A long silence ensued while the two of them seemed to bond. Jessica sensed a strong connection to Eli's mother.

Annie knelt next to Jessica and focused her attention on the chest. "You're the only other person who's ever looked inside of this chest."

"Oh . . ."

"But I really want you to see it. Your great-uncle . . ." Annie caught her emotion before it got away from her. "I miss him dearly. He gave me advice, even till the end. Throughout my life, especially when I knew I was in love with Levi and thought I had to let him go . . . your uncle gave me his very best wisdom. And I'll always be grateful." She caught an emotional breath. "In fact, when something bothers me and I need an answer, I think of going to his barn to talk to him." She smiled a little while offering a helpless shrug. "Of course, I can't. But his memory . . . excuse me."

Annie stepped away for a tissue. She blew her nose and returned to Jessica. She cleared her throat and squared her shoulders. "I feel so blessed, Jessica, to have known your great-uncle. And all the love he showed me . . . I want to give that back to you."

Jessica's jaw dropped; she wasn't sure how to react to such kindness. All her life, no one had ever made her feel so important. So loved. She wondered what to say to reciprocate.

She wasn't sure, so she didn't respond. Instead, she enjoyed the wonderful sensation that swept through her chest. As she contemplated how generous Annie Miller was, the thought of selling the house entered her thoughts until her head began to ache. Jessica's close connection to the Miller family certainly muddied her desire to sell Sam's property and then leave. They had welcomed her with open arms and had made her feel like she was one of them.

The happiness Jessica had just experienced was quickly replaced with guilt. It was easy to see that this small town meant much more to its people than just a dwelling place. The folks appeared emotionally connected, as if this town was part of them.

"Jessica?" Annie's soft voice interrupted Jessica's chaotic thoughts. "Something's bothering you. You're frowning. And your hands are shaking."

Jessica glanced at Annie before shamefully looking down at the floor. When Jessica looked up again, she struggled to find her voice. She felt she owed Annie Miller some sort of explanation for selling.

"You want to talk about it?"

After offering a light shrug of her shoulders, Jessica swallowed and nodded her head and stood.

Annie followed suit and motioned to the bed. Jessica sat at the edge and Annie claimed the spot next to her. They turned to each other so that their knees nearly touched.

"Whatever you do, please don't let anything bother you, Jessica." Annie remembered something and sat up straighter. "Old Sam always used to tell us girls to never let anything steal our joy. That today is a gift only God can give to us. And we can't ever take back the moment."

"Annie, right now, I'm torn."

Annie lifted a curious brow and continued to study the concern on this young girl's face.

"I know how much Pebble Creek means to you. To your family. Eli was the first to mention it when we met. And here I am, doing everything I can to sell what's so dear to your hearts."

Annie took Jessica's hand in hers and locked gazes with the young girl. "Jessica, Old Sam left the land to you." A slight smile lifted the corners of her lips as she raised her palms in a helpless gesture. "There's a reason for everything. Of course, we don't know what it is. But Jessica . . ." She reached out and squeezed Jessica's fingers with affection. "God's plan for us is way beyond our knowledge. He's the only one who knows the end result. And what I'm sure of is that family was more important than anything to Old Sam. And he'd want a family to live in his home, enjoy Pebble Creek, and continue making memories. Of that, I have no doubt. And you'll make that happen. Some wonderful family will carry on the happiness that was born at Pebble Creek."

Jessica let out a sigh and seemed to relax a little. "From what I know about my great-uncle, he was all about family. But the sale of the property . . ." She looked away a moment before refocusing her attention to Annie. "With the money, I'll be able to buy a place close to my job. Right now, I live on the other side of the city, and it takes me over an hour to get to work. I can't imagine how less stressful my life will be when I'm close. And what makes this more difficult is that we are close to getting an offer . . ." Her voice cracked with emotion.

As Annie became unusually still, a nervous laugh escaped Jessica's throat, and she shook her head in disbelief. "Annie, I know we've all got problems, but I have trouble dealing with stress. In fact, I've had issues I didn't think I could cope with."

Annie pressed her lips together thoughtfully.

"But knowing that soon that stress will be gone, I feel so much relief."

Several thoughtful heartbeats later, Annie nodded. "I understand, Jessica. I can't imagine what it would be like living in the city, let alone having to get to work every morning in traffic. Sometimes I take for granted what I have here."

Jessica looked at her to continue.

"I have everything I need. Every once in a while, something comes up that requires prayer. But I feel fortunate that God has given me my wonderful family and the best life I could ever imagine out here in the country. Jessica, when you go to bed at night, say your prayers. Ask God to help you make decisions. And if you trust in Him, nothing will worry you. Because He created you."

Jessica contemplated Annie's words.

"Look at it this way. Remember the delicious chocolate cake that Rebecca made for the fish fry?"

Jessica nodded.

"That cake didn't just come about. Rebecca had to add the right ingredients and mix them together. It's the same way with people."

"You think?"

"Of course. Just like the cake, we couldn't come about by chance. There's no way." The corners of Annie's lips lifted into a gentle smile. "Think about it, Jessica. God made us all. And we live for Him."

That evening, rain beat against Old Sam's roof. A bright bolt of lightning prompted Jessica to make her way to the bedroom window and look out.

For sure, Old Sam's flowers were getting plenty of water. Loud thunder crackled. She startled, but knew that she was safe inside Old Sam's home and that the Millers weren't far away, if she needed them. But tonight, her heart pumped at an uneasy speed. Her hands shook.

She went to the kitchen and swallowed a pill that she pulled from a container in her makeup bag. She frowned. She didn't like relying on medicine. But as she drifted back to the afternoon, her chest ached until she thought she would be sick.

She thought of her time with Annie. When Jessica had confessed her guilt about selling, she hadn't gathered enough courage to actually say that the interested party didn't even have a family. Or that he didn't plan to live at Pebble Creek.

She considered the kindness the Miller family showed her. At the same time, she recalled the big offer that was about to materialize. That the man who wanted her place for a vacation getaway was a far cry from the family that the Millers wanted.

Breathing in relief that the pill wouldn't take long to work, she went to bed and propped her feet up. Taking deep breaths, she closed her eyes and tried to relax.

As she lay on the simple but comfortable bedding, she thought of Old Sam and yearned to know him. She opened her eyes and frowned, pressing a finger against her chin.

As the pleasant scent of oak filled her nostrils, she smiled a little. She closed her eyes again and began to relax, but the moment she thought about selling to someone who wouldn't even live here, the ache worsened.

The next thought that came along was Annie's theory that people couldn't have happened without a Creator. The analogy of the cake made sense.

Jessica wanted to believe in God. She hadn't been a bad person, not by her standards anyway. But she still wasn't convinced He existed.

She sat up and paced while her thoughts wandered to her younger years, a time she'd rather forget. But the moment her gaze landed on her great-uncle's key on the near-by desk, she forgot everything that was driving her crazy and started imagining what the key unlocked.

Old Sam, what did you make for your wife? She stood to retrieve the key, studied it, and held it between her fingers.

Old Sam, I love you even though I've never met you. You stunned me by leaving me Pebble Creek. I don't deserve your kindness and generosity. But as I learn about you, I have a hunch that you want me to find your gift for Esther. And my curiosity won't let it go.

She held the unique-looking metal in front of her and wondered. *Where is it?*

The following afternoon, Jessica waved good-bye as Eli, Wayne, and Chuck stepped out of the front entrance and closed the door. When the lock clicked, she hugged her hands to her hips and focused on the kitchen.

She let out a sigh and quick steps took her to the side porch where she grabbed a broom and a dustpan. She adjusted the fan to hit her and began sweeping the floor.

She whistled while she did so. To her amazement, she'd been thinking much less about her job and her horrendous commute to work. Instead, the conversation she'd had with Eli's kind mother continued to absorb her thoughts, prompting a smile. At the same time, Mary's theory that each flower couldn't have happened without a Designer flitted through her head.

She admired both women. According to Annie, everything good came from God, and there was no problem too small or too large for Him.

Since their conversation, Jessica had thought about asking the Lord for guidance. Obviously, it worked for Mary. For Eli. And Annie.

As she breathed in the pleasant scent of fresh cut wood, she considered Annie Miller and her strong faith.

I would love to be half as satisfied with my life as she is with hers. How wonderful it would be to just hand my problems over to someone and trust that I'm taken care of. But how realistic is it?

There must be something to it if the Miller family believes it. She thought of Old Sam's Bible as she glanced down at the large pile of dust and knelt. She swept the debris into the dustpan and made her way to the trash can, where she emptied the dirt.

So many things filled her mind that she closed her eyes to calm herself. Eli. Annie. Mary. Praying to God for guidance. Selling Old Sam's place to the right people. Purchasing a place of her own near her work. The key.

A sudden beep prompted her to glance at her phone. Jessica stopped her task at hand and answered.

"Jess, it's Sandy. Great news! The buyer I told you about has made an offer on your property! It's more money than I ever imagined we'd get." Jessica closed her eyes and swallowed a hard knot that blocked her throat.

"Jessica? Are you there?"

The following morning, Eli glanced at Jessica. Since he'd started work, they'd barely said two words. In fact, she hadn't offered him iced tea.

Something's wrong. She's avoiding me.

Chuck put down his hammer and interrupted Eli's thoughts. "Time for a break." Eli agreed.

But instead of heading to the pickup truck for water, he made his way to Old Sam's flower bed, where Jessica was touching a new green leaf on Old Sam's rosebush.

"It's coming back."

Jessica got up from her squatting position and smiled. "Mary gave it a special formula." She lifted her palms. "And look!"

Together, they bent to marvel at the green that had started to appear. But Eli wasn't here to talk about the rosebush. He cleared his throat and spoke in a low, serious tone. "Something's wrong, Jessica. Want to talk about it?"

* * *

Later that afternoon, Jessica walked alongside Eli as they climbed the hill that overlooked Pebble Creek. The pressure to sell the property to the businessman so she could get rid of the stress of driving through the city was causing as much stress as the actual drive across St. Louis to work. A knot pained the back of her neck. She stopped to catch her breath.

"Okay, let's have it." A combination of sympathy and urgency edged Eli's voice.

"Thanks for taking off early to talk to me."

"It actually worked out well. The tile needs to set before we step on it again." After a short pause, he nudged her arm to avoid stepping in a dip in the ground. "Something's bothering you. You've avoided me all morning. You didn't even offer me tea."

Jessica wanted to talk to him about the sale of Pebble Creek. About the turmoil inside of her that she would displease the Millers. She closed her eyes and took a deep breath. But anxiety had already started to set in.

"Jess?"

Deciding on a straightforward approach, she started to explain the offer. She went on to tell about the man who wanted to buy it. About the pressure she faced at selling to someone who didn't intend to live there or raise a family there. At the end, she waited for a response from Eli, her heart picking up speed.

For long moments, the only sound was their breathing as they continued up the hill. Suddenly, emotions hit her from every direction, and she lowered her gaze to the ground so Eli wouldn't see her tears.

Jessica's lungs started pumping harder and harder for

air until she lay down on her back on the dirt trail and closed her eyes. Light-headedness began to set in. "Eli, I need your help."

He knelt beside her. "Are you okay?"

"I will be. Hold my feet up."

Without wasting time, he followed directions while she closed her eyes and tried for slow breaths. She silently began counting down from a hundred, like her doctor had told her to do when a panic attack came on. When she finally managed to steady her breathing, she opened her eyes and focused on his face. Tiny lines around his eyes revealed great concern. His jaw was set.

"Are you okay?"

"Please. Just prop my legs up a little longer."

He nodded.

Finally, the light-headedness ceased, and Jessica looked at Eli and smiled in relief. "Eli, I get panic attacks. They started when I was a kid when my dad got drunk." She swallowed. "When I had to hide from him."

To her relief, Eli didn't respond. He continued to listen.

"At home, in St. Louis, I take medicine to prevent the attacks from happening. I think I mentioned that to you. But now the anxiety is coming back . . . because of the offer and because I don't want to displease you and your family. Or Old Sam." A couple of tears slid down her cheek.

She drew her legs closer to her body and sat up. There was still no response from Eli as he knelt beside her.

"It's okay, Jessica. Please. Don't worry. I can't stand to see you so uneasy. Life is too short. Maemm always tells us what Old Sam once told her. That today's a blessing from God. To enjoy it. Because once it's over, we can't have it back."

Jessica lifted her chin and studied the gentle man next to her. "Eli, being with you and talking to you"—she let out a relieved breath—"is so comforting. Thank you for listening to me. For everything. Your mother told me the same thing. Oh, Eli, if only I could be so happy as you are. As your mother is."

His eyes gleamed with moisture as their gazes locked. He lowered his voice to a whisper. "You can, Jessica. It's all about knowing God. Believing in His purpose for you."

She paused and considered Eli's words. Finally, she was more curious about Eli's God than ever. "If there is a God, what do you think His purpose is for me, Eli?"

He studied her, and moments later, his lips curved in amusement.

"What?" she asked.

He chuckled. "I'm not sure, Jessica Beachy, but I'm certain of His purpose for me."

She looked at him to continue.

"To keep you out of trouble."

She smiled and relaxed. "I know I've probably been a bit of a worry."

He said softly, "But it's more than that, Jessica." He shook his head before focusing on her face. "Since you've moved into Old Sam's home, I've become aware of a great purpose God has given me." He stopped as if deciding what to say next. "It's to make sure you know your Lord and Savior. And when that happens . . ." He lifted his palms to the sky.

"The sale of your house . . . driving across the city to get to work . . . these things won't matter like they do now. Because if you look at the whole picture, if God guides your life, He's really all that matters. And you'll trust Him."

As she absorbed his potent words, he continued. "Over the years, Maemm and I have had a lot of conversations about God. How to live our lives. You know what she always told me?" He went on with a wry smile. "You'll be very interested in this because she heard it from your great-uncle."

She sat up a little straighter. "What?"

"That only God is privy to everything that happens in our lives. From birth to death. And that each time something happens, good or bad, there's a reason for it. But only He knows the end result."

"That's interesting."

"Jessica, pray to do the right thing. I know God is watching over you." Eli winked. "He brought you to us, didn't He?"

Jessica nodded.

"There's something I feel compelled to share with you. It's about what I've noticed since you've come to Pebble Creek."

She looked at him to continue.

"You've changed a lot."

"I have?"

Eli offered a confident nod. "With the exception of today, since we've first met, you've become more relaxed. And I like it when you wear jeans and tennis shoes. I was worried that you'd fall in those heels."

She laughed. "Over all, I have been much more relaxed than ususal."

"Doesn't that tell you something?"

She considered his question. "Like what?"

"Like maybe you should rethink the sale. At least, who you're selling to. You said yourself that's what brought your stress back." He stood, and she followed suit.

The strength of what Eli had just said stunned her so much that she couldn't find words to respond. She wondered what would happen if she declined the sale. Even more, if she stayed here at Pebble Creek.

She quickly decided it wasn't plausible. How would she make a living? What would she do in this quiet, uneventful countryside? To her knowledge, there weren't any hotels in the area where she could work.

Then something came to her. A realization that nearly took her breath away. As they began climbing up the hill again, she spoke in a soft, vulnerable voice. "Eli, you truly care about me."

When he didn't respond, she decided to go on. At this point, she knew she could speak her mind and that Eli wouldn't pass judgment on her. "No one has ever cared about me the way that you do. Like your family does. And to be honest, what I'm feeling . . ." She drew her hand to her chest. "I don't even know what to think. I just want to thank you."

In silence, they neared the top. Eli motioned and let out a breath. "There they are. The stones my parents sat on when they were kids."

Together they stood and looked down at the creek. While they did so, the gentle breeze lifted the ends of Jessica's hair. She shoved it back over her ears. The creek below them prompted her to draw in a breath that was the epitome of awe.

A strange sense of calmness filled her, despite the heavy conversation she and Eli had just had.

"I understand why Maemm and Daed used to walk all the way up here."

"Me too."

They bent to sit on the stones. But the small garden of coneflowers behind Annie's and Levi's stones drew Jessica's attention, and she knelt to touch one of the purple centers.

Beside her, Eli did the same. "It's beautiful isn't it?"

"Mm-hmm."

"But it seems like a strange place for a flower bed."

From her peripheral vision, Jessica glimpsed Eli squinting.

Jessica grinned. "No, it doesn't. Not if this was his and Esther's favorite spot." She lowered her voice. "The very place my great-uncle asked Esther to marry him."

She bent closer. The bright sunlight hit the patch of flowers, and she saw something shiny at the base of the leaves.

Without saying anything, she squinted for a better look at the copper. When she glanced over at Eli, his attention was focused on the same thing.

Eli began brushing away dirt to uncover the object. He removed enough so they could detect the outline of the box.

Jessica didn't take her gaze off of the object. "Is it copper?"

Several seconds later, Eli nodded in agreement. "I think so. The ground is soft from the rain, but I need a shovel. Let's come back tomorrow and dig up whatever it is."

In a low, certain tone, Jessica spoke. "Whatever it is, the key will unlock it. I know it."

Leaning back, Eli brushed his hands together, and tiny

pieces of mud dropped to the ground. "You're determined, aren't you?"

She nodded.

"I don't want you to be disappointed if the key doesn't work."

Standing, she looked down at the copper that had been partially exposed. "Tomorrow, we'll find out what Old Sam's key unlocks and what's inside that." She pointed.

Jessica's heart picked up speed as her mind wandered to Old Sam. Whatever he'd buried had been important enough to carry it all the way to the top of this hill and place it between Levi's and Annie's sitting stones.

Suddenly, something disturbed her. She tensed and crossed her arms across her chest.

"Something wrong?"

"Eli, I just had a disturbing thought. What if the key *won't* open the box?"

Eli rolled his eyes and offered a conciliatory shrug of his shoulders. "Then it won't."

She tapped the toe of her tennis shoe against the stone. "That's not what I meant."

"Then what did you mean?"

She harrumphed. "I know that the key goes to whatever we'll uncover tomorrow. But what if the lock is rusted? Esther's been gone a long time . . . which means that whatever is buried has been in the ground for years."

The thoughtful expression in his eyes made her smile. She was fairly certain that the man opposite her did not believe the key opened this box. The box that Old Sam had buried. His skepticism showed in his voice.

As they faced each other, Eli seemed even taller than usual. The sun hitting his face made his eyes take on a lighter shade of hazel. The color was so beautiful, it reminded her of the oak leaves behind her apartment complex in the fall. Of cinnamon in her spice box.

He took a deep, thoughtful breath and pushed it out. "Tomorrow, we'll know."

"We'll just have to be patient, won't we?"

He offered a firm nod. At the same time, as if on cue, they turned toward the creek. At that moment, Jessica felt a sense of great satisfaction.

As if reading her thoughts, Eli said in a low voice, tinged with emotion, "Now I understand why this was my parents' special spot."

Jessica took in the captivating stream below, country houses spread out acres apart, and imagined Annie and Levi Miller running up and down this very hill when they were young.

"They must have taken a lot of breaks while they hauled these stones. I wonder what they talked about when they came up here."

Old Sam, if only I had met you. My life would have been different. For the better. I know you would have protected me.

Eli cleared his throat. "Jess?"

The way he said her abbreviated name with such softness made her pulse pick up speed. This time, she didn't even bother to scold herself.

She merely looked at him in silence as she enjoyed their togetherness.

He bent closer. He was so near, she could feel his warm breath. "You can stay here, you know."

A long silence ensued while she gave great consideration to his statement. And she realized more than ever that she could never live here and watch this wonderful man marry a nice Amish girl. That startling realization made her stiffen.

No. This can't be happening.

To her dismay, he pursued the subject. "Jess, your life can be whatever you want it to be. Old Sam once told me that. You've been through a lot, but learn from it. In fact, use it to your advantage. You might feel like you don't have control over what happened, but you do. And to have a happy life, the kind you really want inside of your heart, you've got to put the past behind you and create your future." He offered a casual lift of his shoulders. "It's up to you. Just think of how happy you've been since you got here. You said yourself that you've been more relaxed since coming here."

Nervously, she tapped the toe of her tennis shoe against the ground. "I know. But staying here isn't that easy, Eli."

"Why not? I'll always be here for you, to help in any way I can. That's a promise."

Jessica's chest rose and fell much too quickly. She hoped he didn't notice. And she was sure that he didn't know how she felt about him. Otherwise he wouldn't have made such a strong commitment. He obviously didn't have a clue that she wanted much more than his help. She yearned for his love. To spend the rest of her life with him.

"I wish your kind, loving God would help me."

She was quick to note the hopeful expression that filled his eyes.

After a slight hesitation, the tone of his voice became even more serious. "He will, Jess. But you've got to ask Him."

"I want to. But I don't know if I can."

He looked at her to go on.

"When did you start to know God?"

She turned and shrugged helplessly as she walked away from him.

But he followed her. She couldn't see him, but she heard him breathing. She heard his boots stepping behind her.

When she stopped, she turned and caught his gaze. She was quick to catch the surprised expression in his dark eyes.

"I can't pinpoint a certain time. Ever since I can remember, my folks have taken me to church. Raised me to pray at the table and at night, by my bed. I just always knew, Jess. I never doubted."

He shoved his thumbs into his pockets and let his fingers rest over the tops. His right foot tapped nervously as he looked directly into her eyes.

"Jess, just think of how complex this world is. For example, feel my heart beat."

She stared at him in surprise. He surely wasn't asking her to touch him. Not that there was anything wrong with that. There wasn't.

But her feelings for him . . . they were so strong, she feared her reaction. The last thing she wanted was for him to know how she felt about him. That would complicate her life even more.

"What?"

He motioned to his chest and offered an encouraging nod. "Go ahead." When she didn't react, he took her fingers in his and pressed them hard against his chest. They were so close, she wondered if he could hear her heart race to an excited, dangerous beat.

"Can you feel my heart pumping?"

Talking would reveal her breathlessness, so she pressed her lips together and merely nodded.

"Did you ever stop and wonder how a heart could beat without a Creator?" He gave a quick shake of his head. "Jess, I'm not a doctor, but I'm fully aware of the complexity of the human body. That when one little thing gets out of sync, the whole body reacts." He raised his voice in excitement. "There's just no way this could be without a Designer!"

Jessica considered his theory and frowned. "What you say makes sense, that's for sure. Just like Mary says a beautiful plant couldn't have just happened. And Annie says the same thing about the delicious chocolate cake at the fish fry."

Eli grinned and paused to take a deep breath.

Fully aware that his hand still covered hers, Jessica stood very still. His warm touch was so comforting and reassuring, she never wanted his fingers to leave hers. It was as if she wore a helmet and no one could hurt her.

"You're making something that's so simple, so hard."

Jessica's lips parted with amazement when he tightened his grip around her fingers and lowered her hand to waist level. To her surprise, he didn't let go. For long, thoughtful moments they looked at each other with a curious intensity. Gray flecks danced in his eyes.

She knew that Amish men didn't hold hands with single women. Yet he was doing just that. The gentleness of his callused palm swept up her arms all the way to her neck.

The tingling sensation stirred a mixture of unfamiliar emotions within her. She yearned to close her eyes and relish the delicious sensation that was an odd combination of comfort and excitement and other things she didn't recognize. It was such a wonderful, new experience, she wanted to shout for joy. When he let go, she missed his warmth and reassurance.

"I . . . I'm sorry, Jess."

She parted her lips in surprise. "For what?"

He swallowed and lowered his gaze to the ground. When he lifted his chin, she noticed his turmoil-filled eyes. They reminded her of the sky just a couple of days ago before the rainstorm hit.

His voice was barely audible. "For holding your hand." Several heartbeats later, he continued. "But I proved my point." He raised his palms, then dropped them.

She didn't mention how his touch had affected her. It might scare him. Yet she certainly didn't want him to feel guilt over something that made her feel so good. "I'm glad you did it."

"You are?"

"Uh-huh." She stammered. "Even if it was only to prove a point."

"I want to change your life, Jess. I want you to know our Lord and Savior. In fact, I yearn for it with everything I have. It's more important to me than breathing."

She processed his words until she recognized their significance.

"What's going on in that head of yours?" Eli's voice broke her reverie.

She gave a gentle lift of her shoulders while he motioned to the sitting stones. There was so much turmoil inside of her, she didn't dare speak. *Will I be able to sort all of this out?*

She tried to make sense of what he wanted. At the same time, she was certain that Eli and his family had what she yearned for. Longed for it so much, she could almost taste it. She wasn't sure why. Before coming here, she hadn't felt as if she missed out on anything.

Maybe her turmoil was due to the contrast between the warm, loving, contented central Illinois folks and her unstable upbringing. They were two different worlds.

For a hopeful moment, she imagined a carefree life. No stress. She wondered what it would be like to not worry about what had happened years ago.

"You're awfully quiet, Jess."

The soft, affectionate way he said her name made her heart jump with excitement. By now, she knew that scolding herself for her reaction didn't do any good. She just couldn't put the lid on her feelings for this young Amish man.

Finally, she found the right words. "Eli, everything about this place . . ." She motioned with her hands and swallowed. "The people here . . . I can't even begin to put into words how wonderful it is." She blinked at the sting of emotional tears. "All my life, I've never known such stability. In fact, I wasn't even aware that other's lives differed so drastically from mine." A nervous laugh escaped her throat.

A long silence ensued before he responded, and when he did, gratitude edged his voice. "I am fortunate, Jess. This type of life is all I've known, so I don't have anything to compare to."

"Consider yourself lucky."

"You think?"

With a sad smile, she nodded. "Before I came here, I was sure I wouldn't like it. I contemplated how I would fit in. And when I learned that Old Sam's house didn't

even have electricity, I was certain I wouldn't survive
without being able to watch television."

After a thoughtful pause, she went on. "But Eli, this . . ."
She extended her arms. "It's everything I could ever
dream of. And"—she blinked at the sting of tears—
"I don't want to leave."

Chapter Nine

That evening, Jessica took off her tennis shoes and propped her feet up on the end of the couch. As she placed her palms under her head, she took in a deep breath and closed her eyes. *Breathe slowly.* As she tried to relax, she smiled a little.

So much happened today. I want to relive every moment. Tomorrow, Eli and I will open the box that my dear great-uncle hid for the woman he loved. What's inside?

As she contemplated that potent question, her thoughts migrated to her walk up the hill with Eli. She crossed her arms over her chest and wiggled her toes. She'd never discussed her health condition with anyone.

But today, she'd openly poured out the details. She'd had to. Otherwise, Eli would have been concerned. As it turned out, she was sure he understood. And his understanding had comforted her like a soft cotton blanket on a cold winter's night.

Her condition wasn't serious; most of the time, she had it under control. She just needed to get enough rest, to eat enough protein, and keep her stress at a minimum.

Tree branches scraped the siding, making a light

squeaking sound. Every once in a while, she could hear the wind howl in the background. She started to relax and stretched her arms over her head. As she did so, a yawn escaped her.

She checked her watch. Normally, it was time for another rerun of *Friends*. She rolled her eyes and smiled as she looked at the perfect spot for a television. But to her surprise, she didn't yearn to watch her favorite show. And since she'd come to Illinois, she hadn't finished one crossword puzzle.

Right now, she preferred to think of Eli. *Eli*. The thought of him prompted her to bring her hands together over her stomach and interlace her fingers. The corners of her lips curved up into a happy grin. How could she be worried about anything when she was with him?

He was the most calm, logical person she'd ever met. To her relief, his demeanor was contagious. In fact, when they were together, she found herself enjoying the moment and forgetting the unstable, chaotic details of her childhood.

When she recalled her palm against his chest, she closed her eyes. She'd never taken time to consider the complexity of the human body. Had Eli any idea how his gentle touch had made her pulse zoom with an odd combination of excitement and calmness? How could two opposite emotions be experienced at the same time?

The moment they'd touched, a strange, blissful sensation of reassurance had overcome her. And to think that he'd actually apologized for it. What he didn't know was how the warmth of his fingers on hers had changed her. *How? I'm not sure. But I'm different.*

Without thinking, she sat up and made her way to

Old Sam's library, where she retrieved the key and held it between her fingers. The metal felt cool against her skin. Her gaze slid to the Holy Bible and the bookmark that stuck out at the top.

Key in hand, she opened the book. She scanned the Scripture in front of her that talked about how Jesus was the Son of God. She took a seat in Old Sam's chair and continued reading.

Perplexed, she stood, returned the Bible to the desk, stuck the bookmark back in, but left the pages open. Eli had told her that he tried to follow God's Word. That eternal life in heaven was there for those who believed in the Lord. That she was making things too hard.

She stepped back to the living room and reclaimed her place on the couch, as she gave great thought to what she'd just read. The contents in small print had piqued her interest enough to finish the chapter.

While she contemplated eternal life and the God that Eli believed in, she recalled her mother's and father's funerals and the Scripture that the pastor had read at their graveside services.

She'd never really wondered what had happened to her parents after they died. Was there a chance that they were in heaven? At home, they'd never discussed God or eternity. But if there was indeed a kind and loving God, would he leave them out?

She closed her eyes. Suddenly exhausted, a mélange of thoughts flitted through her mind until she stood and returned to the library, to the Bible and to the mysterious key next to it.

She yearned for the same contentment Eli had. But how could that very happiness belong to her if she didn't believe? If God existed, would He enter her heart and claim her as one of His own?

This metal key will open Sam's gift. But the key to true happiness and eternal life . . . is it God?

That evening, Jessica knelt at the side of Old Sam's bed and folded her hands in prayer. As she closed her eyes, she focused on what Eli had told her to do. To pray for guidance. That in the end, knowing God was all that mattered.

Her fingers shook. So did her knees. In a soft plea, she spoke. "Dear God, if You are there, please let me know. I need someone to watch over me and to guide me to make the right decisions. I need You."

When she opened her eyes, she rose and slid into bed, placing the Bible next to her. She thought of Eli's heart. As she considered the complexity of the human body, she agreed with Eli. It couldn't have just happened by chance.

She considered Mary's theory about plants and the way she'd described her favorite rose having a different color at the tip. *That couldn't have just happened, either.*

She turned onto her side, closed her eyes, and hoped that if God was truly there, He would help her to make the right decisions. She acknowledged that right now, she had more choices than she'd ever had.

As she stretched, she also acknowledged that she didn't look forward to returning to work and purchasing the house of her dreams. Agony filled her chest at the thought of leaving her great-uncle's place and never seeing the Millers again. Of not being able to look at Pebble Creek from her living room window.

This place wasn't close to work. Or in St. Louis. Still, she couldn't imagine not being here.

She finally had an offer that would allow her to do what she'd yearned to do. The tremendous stress of driving through the city every morning would finally be gone. She loved her job and didn't want to give it up. Yet why did the mere thought of moving away from this particular house devastate her?

She'd lived without believing in God her entire life, and she'd never missed Him. Yet now, her yearning to know Him was so very strong, and she wondered if He really did exist.

Okay. I want to live close to work. The businessman who will purchase Pebble Creek will enable that to come true. At the same time, what benefits me, disappoints my new family. The Millers. It also disappoints me.

Her jaw dropped at that admission. Were they indeed family? *Her* family? *Yes, they are.*

Jessica frowned and clenched her hands together. By now, she truly loved her great-uncle and considered him a vital part of her life. How could she go through with the sale, knowing that it would have disappointed him? *Did he intend for me to live here?*

Her thoughts flitted to Eli's strong belief in God. She stiffened and pressed her lips together thoughtfully. What Eli had told her about the birth of Jesus and the resurrection on the cross tugged at her emotions.

For sure, it was a great story. But how could she know it was real? That God was real? How could she know that the Bible wasn't just full of stories that people liked to hear and believe?

Again, she considered the beating of Eli's heart. A sigh escaped her throat as she acknowledged that there was no way the brain and the heart and everything else that went into allowing her to breathe could just have happened without a Creator.

She vividly recalled the interesting discussion she'd had with Mary, and the bright girl's theory of the intricate design of a plant. That the details had to have been created.

Suddenly, exhaustion hit her as her head rested on the pillow. Turning on her side, she eyed the Bible until her lids closed.

Breathing in, she fell into a deep sleep. And in her dreams, she imagined the disappointment on her great-uncle's face when the home he'd loved so very much fell into the hands of someone who didn't even live here. She envisioned the empty house.

As she did so, Eli Miller's face appeared. As she studied his eyes, she regretted everything she was doing. Jessica tossed and turned. So many things suddenly made sense. Mary was right about plants. They had to have been designed by someone. And Eli's heart . . . any heart, including her own, had to have been created. There's no way the complexity of the human body could have just happened.

She opened her eyes and sat up. Her heart suddenly pounded with ferocity. She drew her hand over it, and when she did, Eli's declaration sank in so that she totally agreed with him. And she agreed with Mary.

Salty tears of happiness and joy stung her eyes, and

she blinked. She bowed her head and pressed her palms together and whispered, "Dear Lord, I know You are there. Please take charge of my life."

The following morning, Eli filled the horse trough with the hose. As Flame sucked up water, Eli chuckled. "You're a thirsty boy."

At five in the morning, the sun was bright, and the temperature was already in the seventies. He wiped moisture from his forehead. Above, a jet left a trail of white in the blue sky. Down the road, a horse pulled a buggy.

A fly buzzed in front of him, and he swatted it away. When the trough filled to the top, he turned off the hose and wound it, placing it on its hook. Inside the barn, he climbed the ladder up to the loft, grasped a bale of straw by the thick twine that held it together, and shoved the heavy pile over the side.

He climbed back down and carried it to the small stable, where he split the twine with his knife and spread the bedding with a rake.

As the metal teeth squeaked on the cement floor, a warm, gentle breeze floated in from the open doors. The doors creaked. For a moment, he stopped to enjoy nature's air-conditioning. In the distance, he glimpsed Pebble Creek. A knot obstructed his throat as he considered the huge change about to occur.

He swallowed, but couldn't get rid of the uncomfortable lump. He could barely see the Beachy house. His work was nearly complete. But not his mission for Jessica to know Christ.

He frowned and pressed his lips together while he worked. It looked as though a businessman was about to pay big money for the land that was so special to Eli and his family. The place Old Sam had once called *home*.

But soon, it wasn't going to be a place for memories. Of endearment. It would merely be a vacation spot for someone who wouldn't appreciate the property's sentimental value.

Reality prompted the corners of those lips to drop another notch, and he ran his hand over his forehead again to rid it of moisture. He looked down at his boots and shook his head. *At this point, it's practically a done deal. No need to worry about something out of my control.*

Of course, the house would never be the same. Oh, it was the same structure, but it was now wired for electricity. He supposed the new owner would want to take down the clothesline. And the barn? Eli shrugged. It was old. Some might consider it an eyesore. Maybe it would be torn down, too. An ache filled his chest.

But he couldn't control how events transpired. Jessica hadn't grown up here. And although she was hungry for information about her great-uncle, she just didn't have memories to make this place as special to her as it was to him and his family.

Eli returned to raking the bedding. As he worked, he recalled vividly what Old Sam used to say about worrying being a waste of time. That life on earth was too short. And not to let anything or anyone rob your happiness. Because you couldn't redo time.

I need to heed his advice. But it's hard.

Every once in a while, his parents walked the length of the creek together and reminisced. And, of course,

Sam hadn't minded that at all, but the new owner— whoever it would be—might not want trespassers. And the buyer might even build on the hill. A chill darted up his spine and made him lift his shoulders to shed the uncomfortable sensation. What would happen was impossible to predict.

Thinking of finishing up the Beachy home prompted him to speed up his task. When he finished, he scooped dirty straw into a nearby cardboard box and returned the rake to its hook on the wall.

Letting out a satisfied breath, he gave Flame one last stroke over his nose. As the gelding snorted satisfaction, Eli offered an affectionate pat on the head. "Lots of things are about to change, boy. Soon there'll be a new guy in Old Sam's house. And Jessica will head back to St. Louis."

He breathed in before lifting his chin a couple of notches in resolve. "Maybe I can talk her into staying. What d'you think?"

As he stepped toward the house, something Old Sam once said came to him, and Eli smiled a little with a newfound hope. He could nearly hear the low timbre of the wise man's voice as he said, *God works in mysterious ways. Never underestimate the power of prayer.*

Nearing the Miller home, it came to him that he had already given up on Jessica staying. A combination of disappointment and determination prompted him to focus on the positive. He prayed a strong, silent prayer for her to stay. And an even stronger prayer that God would fill her heart with His love and that she'd know Him as her Lord and Savior.

Old Sam's words of wisdom vibrated in Eli's thoughts.

But time was running out. At least, for her to live here.
But as far as Eli's prayers for Jessica to believe in the
Creator of the universe?

He squared his shoulders and opened the side entrance.
As he breathed in the enticing smell of Maemm's yeast
dough floating through the open kitchen window, he
smiled.

"I had given up, Old Sam. Until just now when I
remembered your words of wisdom." *Never underestimate the power of prayer. Now I'm determined more
than ever to keep Jessica here. I know that your great-
niece and I have some great differences, but with God,
anything is possible. And I'll never forget the power of
prayer again.*

He closed his eyes and pressed his palms together.
And prayed.

Later that morning, all Jessica could think about
was God and how He'd already changed her life. She
couldn't wait to tell Eli. When she heard two knocks on
the door, she rushed to the entrance where she turned the
door knob and met Eli's wide smile.

"Come in."

As he stepped inside, he eyed her. "Are you ready
for this?"

Jessica led him to the table. "Iced tea before we go?"

He smiled. "Sounds good."

While Jessica poured the beverages, Eli pulled a chair
out from the dining room table and stretched his legs.
When she came toward him, she glimpsed approval in
his eyes.

"I think Old Sam would like the kitchen."

"Really?"

"*Jah*."

"I love it, Eli." She handed him a plastic glass.

"*Denki*. You're really excited about this, aren't you?" Before she could get a word in, he went on. "Today your face is glowing. There's an excitement I've never seen in your eyes."

"I can't wait to see what's inside the box. But Eli, I have something to tell you." She looked down to choose her words. When their gazes locked, happiness edged her voice. "During our walk yesterday, you gave me a lot to think about."

She drew a hand over her chest and took in a breath. "I went to bed last night thinking about eternal life. About God."

She was quick to note the seriousness in his eyes. He stayed very still while she went on.

"Eli, I couldn't forget what you said about the human body. About your heart." She drew in a breath. "And I prayed. At some point during the night . . . I just knew. Of course, God exists. How could I ever have doubted?"

Without hesitation, he jumped up from his seat and moved around the table to hug her. She held on to him tightly. When they embraced, she knew she never wanted to let him go.

When he released her, his eyes sparkled with moisture. "Jess, you don't know how this makes me feel. I've been praying for you to know Christ. I've wanted it more than I've ever yearned for anything in my life."

Her jaw dropped while she considered his strong words. Slow steps returned him to his chair, and they smiled at each other. A long silence passed while she enjoyed knowing that she was a Christian and what it meant.

Eli broke the silence. "This morning, something Old Sam used to tell me kept playing in my mind."

"What?"

"That with God, nothing is impossible. To pray and to believe."

She took a drink, then scooted her chair closer to the table. "I'm still digesting that God is real." She wasn't sure why she laughed. "Eli, I have so many questions, but there's one thing I'm sure of. God brought me here to know Him. I'm not sure how my great-uncle knew this would happen, but I believe he did."

Eli leaned forward and softened his voice. "Let's get that key and go see what it opens. I know that you're sorting everything out. And the truth is, Jessica, so am I."

Sometime later, Jessica walked ahead of Eli as they made their way up the hill that overlooked Pebble Creek. The humidity made Jessica's T-shirt stick to her back. She ran her finger over her ear to keep hair out of her face.

As she took in the beauty of the property, she realized that God had created this entire place. That it hadn't just happened. No, Pebble Creek was no coincidence. And she owed her new life to Old Sam. And to the Millers.

Eli's voice broke her reverie. "I just want to warn you," he said in a lowered voice. "We can't be sure that your key will unlock whatever's in the ground. I don't want you to be disappointed."

His conservative approach didn't stymie her excitement one bit. She put her hands on her hips and raised her chin to counter his skeptical gaze when he turned to her. "I will *not* be disappointed! Eli Miller, I know we're going to find Old Sam's gift for Esther!"

After a pause, he chuckled. "I like your positive spirit! That's one of the many things I admire about you."

She absorbed his kind words and swallowed an emotional knot. Today, she felt more special than ever. Not only because of Eli, but because she knew God was watching over her. She had a Heavenly Father who loved her and who had created her. There was no doubt in her mind.

She realized Eli was waiting for her to respond. "Where's your sense of adventure? It's okay to be cautious, I guess, but are you even the slightest excited about finding out what's in the box?"

Stepping to her side, he looked down at her and grinned.

She asked, "You want me to take a turn carrying that shovel?"

When he didn't respond, she took that as a no.

"Just thought I'd offer." She breathed in as she avoided a dip in the ground. "You know, I never realized how good life could be." She shook her head. "But there's a lot on my mind right now. Eli, you know what scares me?"

"What?"

"That my parents . . ." She choked and quickly regained her composure. "They didn't go to church. I don't think they believed." She softened her tone so she could barely hear her words. "I want them to be in heaven."

After a long pause, Eli responded. "Jessica, God is kind and loving. He's also forgiving."

She nodded and smiled a little. "Eli, I don't know what to do about selling Pebble Creek."

He didn't reply.

"I want to do the right thing for God. For Old Sam.

I'd love to live here. Right here on this beautiful land. But my life's in St. Louis. It's where I work."

She noticed the heavy silence that followed. As their slow steps continued up the hill, she considered what she'd just said. She'd been honest.

However, to her surprise, she didn't totally rule out living here. In fact, the idea prompted more serious thinking.

But there were things to consider. For instance, her love for Eli. She drew in a sudden breath at her unexpected revelation. She did love him. She was sure of it.

But after Eli finished the repairs on her home, if she remained here, would she even see him again? That question prompted an ache in her stomach and she frowned.

So many things flitted through her head, she wasn't watching where she was going, and her foot got stuck in a hole. As she nearly tripped, Eli was quick to steady her until she got her balance. Again, his warm, gentle touch made her ache for more. She needed Eli like she needed air.

"Thanks," she said in a soft voice. "I wasn't paying attention."

"That's because you aren't sure you're doing the right thing, Jess."

His words stopped her thoughts until he took her arm and pulled her to face him. When she looked into his eyes, she glimpsed turmoil. But she guessed that his uneasiness wasn't because he loved her. It all had to do with Pebble Creek. Old Sam's land meant everything to him. It wasn't that he wanted her to stay.

"What's going on underneath all of that honey-blond hair, Jess? Are you thinking about my suggestion?"

She hesitated before responding. "You mean, for me to stay here?"

He nodded.

"I've considered it. But a move from another state . . . it's all so complicated."

"Why does it have to be?"

She shrugged. "What would I do for a living?" She looked up at him, then lowered her lids. She could feel warmth flood her cheeks. "Besides, it's not like we'd be seeing each other every day." She hesitated before softening her voice. "Your work's almost done."

When he didn't respond, she thought it odd that her words seemed to disturb him. He didn't say a word, but she sensed uncertainty in his body language. In the fixed straight line of his lips. In his set jaw. The expression in his eyes was cold.

But why would he care if she stayed? The remodeling of her home would be finished, and there would no longer be a need for his services.

Finally, he broke the silence with a low whistle. They both stopped and stared down at Pebble Creek. "Would you look at that?"

She let out a breath of amazement and nodded. "It's got to be the most beautiful place in the world, not that I have anything to compare it to."

"We don't need anything to compare it to. In my heart, I know there's no place like it, and that's the very reason my parents bonded here. For some reason . . ."

He turned to her. Not sure what to say, she merely stared back. Something stirred within her, causing an odd combination of discomfort and bliss. She'd never experienced this kind of sensation and wasn't sure she liked it. Their gazes continued to lock with a curious intensity.

When he turned to proceed up the hill, she felt a sense of loss. The moment they had just shared was so special, she never wanted to forget it. But had it meant anything to him? She focused on making it up the hill. She remembered their reason for this walk and smiled a little. What was inside the box? What would the key reveal?

A newfound enthusiasm edged her voice. "I can't wait to unlock the box." She reached into her right pocket to make sure the unique-looking key was still there. She sighed with relief when she touched it.

For some reason, her fingers on the metal prompted her to think of the Holy Bible in Sam's bedroom and the magazine of daily devotions. She decided to mention it. "Eli, I've read parts of Old Sam's Bible. Scripture."

Eli slowed his pace and glanced down at her without saying anything.

A laugh escaped her throat. She wasn't sure why. There certainly wasn't anything funny about the Bible. Or about reading it. "Now I understand why Old Sam was so wonderful. If he lived by what he read, it certainly explains why everyone loved him."

"So how much have you read?"

"Bits and pieces. About how God so loved the world that he gave his Son. That there are three gifts, and the greatest is love. Stories about Abraham. The first night I was here, I opened the book to where Sam's marker was. It was the book of John."

As the incline steepened, their steps slowed. "I guess it was impossible for me to live in Old Sam's house and not believe. There's so much to learn. In fact, I feel like life's just beginning."

Near the top, Eli stopped and put down the shovel, catching his breath. For long moments, they gazed at each other with what seemed to be a mutual understanding. In the background, the damp breeze caressed Jessica's neck. A honeybee buzzed around her head. All the while, Pebble Creek loomed in the distance.

"Jess?"

"What?"

"I'm so happy that you believe. God must love you terribly, and I know how much it would mean to Old Sam for you to know our Lord and Savior. I wish he was with us right now."

They continued in silence, the only sounds their footsteps, their breathing, and an occasional honeybee buzzing. At the top Jessica and Eli turned to look at each other.

Without words, she looked on as he grabbed the shovel and began digging. As he worked, the light smell of flowers filled Jessica's senses. The scent was pleasant, and the purple on the coneflowers was the most beautiful hue she'd ever seen. Jessica couldn't help but think that the tiny plants served as a nice backdrop for Levi's and Annie's sitting stones.

Jessica took a step back as Eli continued shoveling. As more of the copper box revealed itself, Jessica raised a curious brow in great anticipation.

Eli straightened to tap the shovel against the earth. "It's definitely copper. And you know what that means?"

She didn't take her gaze from the box. "What?"

"That whatever Old Sam put inside must be extremely dear to his heart. That he wanted to make sure his gift would be protected."

Eli continued digging. Finally, the entire container was exposed. Eli had shoveled enough dirt to pull the box out of the earth.

As he did so, two earth worms scurried away. A butterfly fluttered in front of them. Eli and Jessica stared in silence at what had been uncovered.

"It's a copper hope chest, Eli."

With one steady motion, Eli bent to grip the box by the two handles on the sides and pulled it straight up out of the hole. Jessica helped to place the chest between them.

Eli bent to blow loose particles of dirt off the copper. Jessica reached in the back pocket of her blue jeans to retrieve the key.

Eli grinned in amusement as she held the metal key. "It's the moment we've waited for." He motioned. "Go ahead, Jess. See if it works."

With great care, she slowly inserted the key into the lock. It went all the way in, and she turned it. As purple coneflowers danced with the breeze, she opened the lid and gasped with surprise.

With great care, Eli helped her to remove a hand-carved pair of hands holding a gold cross.

Jessica had her left hand on it, and Eli held it with his right. As they focused on Old Sam's work of love, time seemed to stand still. The only sound was that of Eli catching his breath.

Long moments passed before Eli's voice cracked with emotion. "I wish Esther had lived to see what Sam made for their sixtieth wedding anniversary."

Emotion edged Jessica's voice as well, as she imagined Old Sam's great love for his wife of nearly six decades. "So romantic."

Eli cleared his throat. "And I believe the cross between the hands signifies that they'll be together forever in eternity."

Eli's words touched Jessica's heart with such ferocity, the emotion took her breath away. She laid her other hand on the gift that must have been carved with such strong love and faith. She studied the gold cross, and tears started down her cheeks.

"Jess? Are you okay?"

Eli was so close to her, she felt his warm breath against her face. When he spoke, compassion filled his voice. "When I glimpsed these hands and the cross, I immediately knew they were intended to represent Old Sam's marriage to Esther and the great love they shared for nearly sixty years." He hesitated before looking into her eyes. "But to me, Jessica Beachy, it means much more."

She took in his words and wondered what he was trying to say.

With one palm on Sam's gift and his other closing on Jessica's, he smiled a little. "I can't believe this is happening, but I have to tell you what I'm thinking." After catching his breath, he whispered, "I feel like these two hands represent the strong bond between us and that the cross represents God in our lives."

It took a few moments for her to absorb what he'd said. When she finally did, her heart jumped with happiness.

"Jess, this is where you belong. I know it. And Old Sam knew it, too. Think about this: I want more than anything to court you and for us to have the kind of relationship that Old Sam had with Esther. A love that will last for an eternity. I want you to join the Amish church."

Her excited heart nearly stopped at his surprising admission.

His voice cracked with emotion. "Will you stay here with me? I love you."

Chapter Ten

Jessica believed in God. That evening, Eli stopped what he was doing to give a prayer of thanks. "Amen."

Then another reality hit him. What had he done this afternoon? He had told Jess that he loved her, and in a roundabout way, committed his future to her. To his dismay, she hadn't responded.

As Eli filled the horse troughs with water, he frowned and considered the day and all that had transpired. As he caught a bead of sweat that dripped down the front of his neck, he pushed out a sigh of uncertainty.

He turned off the spigot. As he wound the hose around its hook, he thought more about Jessica, her belief in God, Old Sam's gift, and Eli's commitment to the Englisch girl. Feeling overwhelmed, he gave a rough shake of his head to settle his thoughts.

He considered Old Sam and the way he had lived his life with such grace and kindness. Even the walk up the hill with Jessica seemed like a blessing from God because she'd shared with him Scriptures she'd read from Old Sam's Bible. Their discussion about God and eternity and her newfound belief had bonded him to her even more strongly than he'd already been.

Eli chuckled. Even when he wasn't here on earth, the old hope-chest maker was still doing good things for others. God had truly blessed him, and in turn, he had blessed others.

He focused on the open door that led from the barn to the pasture and smiled a little when he glimpsed their two horses. He considered the carefree lives of Flame and Storm; at least he didn't think that they worried about anything. They were well cared for.

He was still happy that God had given him independence. However, right now he wasn't sure he was making good decisions. Before telling Jessica that he loved her, he should have given much more thought to his statement and to the impact it would have on her. She'd been through so much. Now he'd just dumped more on her.

Besides, before today, he'd never even contemplated a future with her. They'd never even courted. And she had just accepted the Lord as her Savior.

Many things needed sorting out. Issues that would take time. She probably hadn't even given any thought to which church she would join. And realistically, a life in the Amish church wasn't even close to the type of life she lived.

The light sound of footsteps interrupted his thoughts and he turned. "Maemm?"

"It's time to eat. I was worried because you didn't come in to say hi after you got back from the Beachy place."

The last thing Eli wanted was to worry his mother. The more he thought about his claim that he loved Jess, the more he became convinced that he'd been out of line and irresponsible.

"Want to talk about it?"

"About what?"

His mother rolled her eyes and smiled as she stepped closer to him. With her gentle hand on his shoulder, she spoke in a soft, reassuring voice. "Whatever's bothering you?"

She pointed a reprimanding finger and smiled. "And don't try to tell me everything's okay because I know it's not." She raised a curious brow. "What happened today between you and Jessica?"

Eli pressed his lips together in deep deliberation and slowly shook his head. There was no use trying to hide things from Maemm. She could read him like a book. And experience had taught him that she was persistent, so there was no use trying to hide what was on his mind.

"I've said something I regret."

Without responding she looked at him to continue.

At the same time, they turned and walked to the bench behind the barn. She took a seat next to him and turned slightly to better face him. "Whatever it is, it can't be that bad. I want to help."

"I'm afraid that this is something that requires Old Sam's wisdom. But he's not here."

The expression on his mother's face was filled with compassion. "Every once in a while, I need him too, Eli. But we don't stay on this earth forever. I learned a little bit from Old Sam. Tell me what's on your mind. Maybe I can help."

Eli cleared his throat and related details of the afternoon.

"Dear Old Sam. He loved Esther so much. Do you know what Jess will do with his gift?"

"I don't know." He held up a hand to stop her from cutting in. "But Maemm, there's more." He went on to tell her about Jessica's newfound belief in God.

Annie Miller pulled in a deep breath. "My goodness, Eli. This could only be God's hand at work." She smiled a little. "And he used our Old Sam to get his task accomplished. What a blessing!"

"It really is. Since I've met Jess, I've taken a personal interest in her." He smiled. "I've been praying for her to know God. She's such a special person and that's why I need to finish telling you about our afternoon."

Eli opened his mouth to speak, but he guessed that his mother was already privy to his thoughts. She'd always had an uncanny ability to know what was on his mind. But she never judged. That was what was so wonderful about her. She and Daed accepted him with unconditional love.

"Maemm, I love Jessica. And I told her."

Eli was quick to note the stunned expression on his mother's face. Her eyes widened with excitement. Her jaw dropped.

In a soft voice, he went on. "I also told her I want to court her and hope she'll stay here."

To his surprise, Maemm grinned.

"What's so funny?"

She wagged a hand in the air and crossed her legs at the knees. "You're so much like me, Eli. It's good, and it's also bad. I've always worn my heart on my sleeve. When I was young, people told me I was much too outspoken and straightforward." She rolled her eyes. "Especially for an Amish girl. That's where you get your directness, I'm afraid."

"Was I out of line?"

His mother swallowed before putting her hand on his. "First of all, let me ask you something. What did she say after you poured out your heart to her?"

He slapped his hands on his thighs and lowered his gaze to his boots, shaking his head. When he lifted his chin, he turned to his mother and shrugged. "Nothing."

His mother frowned. She tapped the toe of her black shoe against the ground and crossed her arms over her lap. "The girl did go through an awful lot this afternoon. Accepting Christ is a life changer."

Annie lowered her voice to an emotional tone. "In the past twenty-four hours, Eli, Jessica Beachy has chosen eternity over death. We need to celebrate! Old Sam would rejoice!"

"But did I ruin it by dumping my feelings on her?" Eli gave an impatient shake of his head. "She already had enough on her mind and in her heart. Why did I go and blurt my feelings for her?"

Annie nodded. "I told you why, Sohn. It's because you've inherited your mother's genes for speaking your mind. But what you said, honey—you didn't do anything wrong. You know that, right?"

Before Eli could respond, his mother stood and began walking very slowly into the barn to the horse trough. As he followed her, he wondered what was going through her head.

With a swift motion, she turned back to face him. "Do you really love her?"

"*Jah.*"

She lifted an inquisitive brow. "Are you sure it's love?

You haven't known her long. And her lifestyle . . . Well, it's much different than ours."

He nodded. "How can I be sure I love her?"

He paced to the fresh bale of hay nearby and returned to meet his mother's skeptical gaze. He lifted his palms. "It's the way I feel when I think of her. I really care for her. I love her enthusiasm. Her caring nature. That's why I've prayed every night for her to know Christ."

He studied her. "How did you know you loved Daed?"

Annie smiled a little. "Let me tell you something, Eli. In my heart, I'm pretty sure I loved him since we were kids. Of course, we met after being apart for a decade, and our lives had changed."

She went on. "I guess you could say our feelings for each other grew. But I was sure I was truly in love with Levi, even though it's something that I had never experienced. I'd been told about it, but love is something you just have to recognize in your own heart. And no one can tell you if you do love or if you don't. It's up to you to figure it out."

She looked away before returning her attention to him. "After Levi came back to town for his cousin's wedding and we spent time together, I was pretty sure I wanted to be with him the rest of my life. So I went to my trusted source for information."

Eli lifted his lips into an amused grin. "Old Sam?"

His mother nodded. "I once asked Old Sam how to know if I really loved your father. Of course, he couldn't give me an answer. I've never really gone into detail about how Levi and I worked out our differences."

Eli frowned. "You mean, because his family had left the community?"

She offered an uncertain shrug. "Actually, it was a little more complicated than that. Anyway, do you know what Old Sam asked me?"

"What?"

"If I loved Levi enough to move away from my parents."

Eli let out a low whistle. As he contemplated what hard decisions his mother had made to be with his father, he sat back and stretched his legs, crossing them at the ankles. At the same time, his mother sat next to him and turned to better face him.

"What did you say?"

"At first"—she shrugged—"nothing." She followed with a roll of her eyes and a half smile. "I didn't have an answer."

Eli swallowed the knot in his throat and realized how very different the world would have been had his parents not married. He wouldn't be here talking to his mother. That made him realize how very important choosing the right spouse was.

Maemm studied her sturdy black shoes for several moments as if deciding how to continue. Finally, she adopted a more thoughtful, serious tone. "I prayed, Eli. I asked God to help me decide what to do, because at first, when your father asked me to spend my life with him, he was Englisch."

"I know the story a little bit." Eli chuckled at the thought of his *daed* driving a car instead of a horse and buggy. His father was such a good Amish role model, Eli couldn't even begin to imagine him being anything else.

"I also kept a journal. In fact, I still do. It's funny, but when I have questions . . ." She paused to let out a small breath and widen her smile. "Because as Old Sam once told me, most of the things that happen to us in this life are out of our control, so how we deal with things really determines who we are."

Eli frowned and nodded. He really hadn't expected this conversation to get so deep. But what his mother was telling him really made sense. And he would give great thought to her words.

"To make a long story short, Levi made a special trip back here to tell me he wanted to join the Amish church and spend the rest of his life with me."

"So your prayers really worked."

"They certainly did." Her eyes glistened with moisture as her voice cracked with emotion. "I can't imagine being with anyone other than Levi, and I'm so happy our story ended the way it did."

He pressed his palms against his thighs.

"So when you think about what you said to Jessica Beachy, consider several things, Eli. Would you move for her? I mean, Sam's great-niece isn't from this area. What if she wanted to be with you and for you to move out of state? Have you even considered that?"

Eli didn't respond. Because he hadn't thought that far ahead.

"And there's so much more to take into consideration, Eli. For instance, the girl just took Christ into her heart. I imagine that she's going through a very complicated process and deciding how she wants to live for our Lord. The Amish church certainly isn't the only church."

Suddenly, Eli realized the complexity of falling in love. Before he confessed his feelings to Jess, he should have given more thought to how their relationship might go.

A gentle hand rested on Eli's shoulder and he locked gazes with the one person he loved most in the world. His mother's voice was soft, yet firm as she stood and looked down at him.

"You're fortunate, Eli. I know this all sounds very complicated, but after you pray on it, you'll know what to do. I'm going to pray about your relationship with Sam's great-niece, too."

Eli stood and looked down with great affection at his mother. "I really jumped the gun, didn't I?"

Her response was a kind, understanding smile. "It doesn't matter." She took his hands in hers and lowered her tone. "Because God guides our lives, and in the end, He'll help you and Jessica to do His will."

God is in charge of my life. Jessica ran an affectionate finger over the cross between the wooden hands. With great appreciation, she placed the art on the end table by her bed and proceeded to retrieve her great-uncle's Bible. She closed her eyes, still trying to digest the significance of what had happened.

She breathed in and relived the moment when she'd acknowledged that God was real. What had happened wasn't her imagination. She'd be a Christian for the rest of her life. She wasn't sure what being a Christ follower entailed, exactly, and the truth was, she knew next to nothing about God's Holy Word.

But now that she realized that she belonged to the Creator of the universe, she couldn't wait to learn everything she could about the One who had control of life on earth and eternity.

Eternity. That very word left her breathless. Light shivers of excitement darted up her arms and landed at the base of her neck. While she sat on Sam's bed and rested the back of her head against the large headboard that touched the wall, she continued reading more of the book of John.

The Bible wasn't easy to understand. She would ask Eli to help her. Within the past twenty-four hours, she'd learned two significant things. Christ loved her. So did Eli.

As she closed the Bible with great care, she felt grateful, but she also recognized that knowing God presented a huge responsibility. There would be a lot to live up to.

What about Eli? He loved her, too. His declaration of his feelings prompted her to close her eyes in bliss and imagine a life with the Amish man she loved with all of her heart.

She hadn't responded to his declaration. Had he expected her to? If she had replied, what would she have told him? She'd been so stunned and so happy, she had been at a loss for words.

Jessica stood and quickly moved to the back of the house, where she gazed at Pebble Creek. Still contemplating Eli Miller's unexpected admission, she opened the door and proceeded to walk outside. As she passed the flower bed, she bent to touch Old Sam's rose that had almost died. *Another miracle.*

From where she stood, she could barely see where the creek curved like an S. As she contemplated the place that meant so much to the Millers, Eli's sincere, honest words floated through her mind until the words morphed into a single message: *I love you. Stay here.*

Many questions flitted through her mind. She wanted to be with Eli. But could she? What would she do for a living? And what about Pebble Creek? She contemplated the contract that needed her signature.

She swallowed an emotional knot. She loved Eli. She had no doubt about that. But there was much more to a relationship than love. He'd asked her to join the Amish church.

As she considered the sacrifices she'd be making, she breathed in and out. *Nothing's wrong with being Amish. But I would have to give up so much. Am I strong enough to do it? I wouldn't even be able to drive my car.*

She whispered, "Dear God, You are in charge of my life. There are so many things I'm unsure of. But what I am certain of is that You'll guide my life in the right direction. Please tell me what to do. Is joining the Amish church what You want of me?"

As she contemplated that question, she made her way back into the house, closed the door, and stepped to the table to look at the contract for the sale of Pebble Creek.

The loud whinny of a horse prompted her to go to the side door. "Annie!"

Jessica rushed to help Eli's mother tie Storm to the post next to the house.

"I'm so glad to see you!" Jessica hugged her. "Annie, I've got so much on my mind. I need to talk. Please, come in."

At the table, Jessica sat opposite Annie. As they drank iced tea, Annie's gaze landed on the contract.

She lifted a curious brow.

Jessica shoved out a defeated breath. "I'm torn. I don't know what to do. I want to stay here with—"

A soft voice cut in. "Eli?"

Jessica nodded.

"Pray. Jessica, when you came to Pebble Creek, you were our miracle. Since then, God has come into your heart. That's the greatest miracle of all. Compared to that, everything else is simple."

Jessica smiled a little. "As always, Annie, you're right." She eyed the contract.

As if reading her mind, Annie spoke in a soft, thoughtful tone. "You'll know what to do about that. But don't act before you're sure you're following your heart. I remember not knowing what the future would bring with Levi and me, but you know what? We never can predict the future. But with prayer, God will guide us." She offered a gentle shrug. "We just have to trust Him."

Jessica stood. "I've got something for you." She made her way to her bedroom and returned with the gift Old Sam had made for Esther.

She handed it to Eli's mother.

When Annie held it, tears slid down her cheeks. "I can't take this, Jessica."

Jessica grinned. "I want you to have it. Because of you and Eli, I've come to love my great-uncle and God."

Jessica closed her eyes and took in an emotional breath. "Annie, I'll miss you!"

Several heartbeats later, Annie set Old Sam's gift on her chair as she stepped to the door. "One moment . . ."

Jessica's gaze followed her, and when Annie came back inside, she held the miniature hope chest Old Sam had made her. She extended her arms to Jessica. "I'll miss you, too . . . if you go." After a slight pause, she whispered, "Here. It's for you."

The following day, Jessica tried to absorb all that had happened since she'd come to Pebble Creek as she fastened her seat belt in her Chevy. She stared at the real estate contract in her hand and smiled before laying it on the passenger seat. This morning, to her amazement, what she needed to do had become crystal clear, thanks to Eli's kind mother. And Old Sam's gift to Esther.

She looked in the rearview mirror while she backed out of the lane, put the car in drive as soon as she reached the blacktop, and headed to Sandy's real estate office. She'd made a commitment. And she'd keep it.

Saturday morning, Jessica sat on one of the stones on the hill overlooking Pebble Creek. As she took in the beauty and the magnificence of the view, she closed her eyes and pressed her hands. "Please guide me." For long moments, she kept her eyes closed and savored her newfound happiness.

The moment she opened them, she glimpsed Eli coming up the hill.

When he joined her, he smiled a little. "I was sure you'd be up here."

"But how did you know?"

He shoved his hands into his trouser pockets and hooked his thumbs over the tops. "Because I knew you wouldn't be able to sign that contract without one final look at Pebble Creek." He motioned to the stone next to hers. "Mind if I join you?"

"I'd love for you to."

Next to him, contentment swept through Jessica's entire body until she felt whole. As always, being near Eli Miller made everything in her life okay. His presence comforted her. Reassured her. She felt secure.

"Eli, I have so much to thank you for. The kitchen . . ." She shook her head. "I don't know what to say. It's beautiful. I could tell halfway through the improvements that it would be hard to leave it when it was finished."

He lowered his gaze. "Jess, that was real nice of you to give Old Sam's gift to Maemm. It means a lot. To all of us."

When she glimpsed him from her peripheral vision, she noticed his fingers shook as he placed his hands on his thighs. He didn't say much, either.

She looked down at the ground. "I took the contract to the real estate agency. Your mother told me to make sure I knew what I wanted before I acted. And I won't ever look back. It's a done deal."

Eli offered a slow nod. A long, thoughtful silence passed while the sun slipped behind a large fluffy cloud. For a moment, the brightness disappeared until the sun escaped the cloud. Finally, Eli spoke in a tone that was so soft, she could barely hear him. And his voice cracked with emotion. "Jessica, please don't go."

She continued to look down at the creek. "Eli, I've given a lot of thought to what you told me. And also about how I feel. And I prayed about what to do."

He smiled a little and turned toward her. "You don't know what it means to me to hear you say that, Jess. That you prayed." After a slight hesitation, he added, "What did you decide?"

She faced him and smiled. "To stay here."

She took in his expression of surprise as he seemed to absorb what she'd said. Then the corners of his lips lifted into a wide grin.

"Would you say that again?"

She raised the pitch of her voice. "I'm staying here, Eli. I tore up the contract. Old Sam's gift for Esther made my mind up to stay. Like I said, when I looked at the cross between the hands, I felt that the gift had really been meant for us. And at that moment, I committed to staying here."

He closed his eyes for several seconds, and when he opened them, she saw his commitment.

She whispered, "Eli, I love you. And I want to be with you. Forever. And to join the Amish church."

With one swift motion, he was on his feet, pulling her up to a standing position. They hugged each other in a tight, emotional embrace. When his arms were around her, the comfort and security that only he could offer enveloped her like a warm blanket. And to her benefit, she never had to leave him. Ever.

When they finally broke their embrace, Jessica explained. "Something your mother told me yesterday stuck in my mind. I knew I loved you. I also was fully aware that becoming Amish wouldn't be easy and that I have so many unanswered questions about the future."

"What did she say?"

"That at one time, she was uncertain about her future with your father. But she knew she loved him. And that's what counted more than anything. And she also knew that God would guide her future."

"Maemm sure got her wisdom from your great-uncle. Jessica, right now, I'm the happiest man on the planet." He grabbed her hands and squeezed them. "I couldn't bear the thought of you leaving. As far as your job . . . don't worry . . . I'll always take care of you, Miss Beachy. With God's help, there's nothing we can't work out."

He cleared his throat. "I love you, Jessica. But there's something else I want you to know."

She parted her lips, waiting for him to go on.

"We haven't known each other long, but you've claimed my heart. And I want to spend the rest of my life with you." He winked. "Jessica Miller has a nice sound to it."

His confession took her breath away. When she finally found her voice, her words came out in a whisper. "Eli, I love you, too. I love your family, Old Sam . . ."

They reclaimed their seats on the stones. The places where Levi and Annie had sat. The very stones that overlooked the creek that had always been so dear to them. And it meant the world to Eli and her, too.

When Eli took Jessica's hand and held it in his, she knew God had helped her to make the right decision. Annie had played a role, of course. And she had Old Sam to thank, too.

"Eli, there's no other man in the world for me. I think Old Sam must have known I'd never be able to leave this place. Or you."

She bent to plant an affectionate kiss on his cheek. "We found Old Sam's secret gift for Esther. But there's another secret at Pebble Creek. One that's become obvious."

He looked at her to continue.

"Love." She extended her arms. "Pebble Creek is all about love. And it's where I want to stay forever. With you."

RETURN TO THE BEGINNING

THE HOPE CHEST OF DREAMS SERIES

Book 1: *Rebecca's Bouquet*

The last thing Rebecca Sommer dreamed her plan to
marry would bring is a heart-wrenching choice. She
thought she and her betrothed, William, would spend
the rest of their lives in Illinois's heartland, raising a
family in their close-knit Amish hometown.
But when he must travel far out of state to save his
ailing father's business, Rebecca braves her relatives'
disapproval—and her own fears—to work by his side.
And though she finds herself ever more in love with
the dedicated, resourceful man he proves to be,
William's growing interest in English ways may be
the one challenge even her steadfast faith can't meet . . .

Book 2: *Annie's Recipe*

Annie Mast and Levi Miller were best friends until his
father was shunned by the church. Now, ten years later,
Levi has returned to Arthur, Illinois, for a brief visit,
and he and Annie discover their bond is as strong as
ever. Spending as much time together as possible,
Annie finds herself dreaming of a future with Levi.
And Levi is soon dreaming of building a home on a
beautiful local hillside—to live in with Annie. Yet their
longings are unlikely to become reality . . .

Book 3: *Rachel's Dream*

Rachel Kauffman and Jarred Zimmerman
seem to have nothing in common.
She's the outgoing youngest of a large, close-knit
Amish clan, and longs to raise a brood of her own near
those she loves. Estranged from his family by tragedy,
Jarred is a young veterinarian who trusts the animals he
heals far more than he trusts people.
However, when Rachel's beloved horse falls ill,
Jarred's struggles to save him show Rachel he's a man
who cares deeply. And the respect he feels for her gentle,
warmhearted ways soon becomes an irresistible bond . . .

Available wherever books and eBooks are sold!

Read on for an excerpt from
Rebecca's Bouquet . . .

His announcement took her by surprise. Rebecca Sommer met William's serious gaze and swallowed. The shadow from his hat made his expression impossible to read.

"You're really leaving?"

He fingered the black felt on the brim. "I know what a shock this is. Believe me, I never expected to hear that Dad had a heart attack."

"Do they expect a full recovery?"

William nodded. "But the docs say it will be a while before he works again. Right now, they can't even guess at a time line. In the meantime, Beth's struggling to take care of him."

While Rebecca considered the news, the warm June breeze rustled the large, ear-shaped leaves on the catalpa tree. The sun peeked from behind a large marshmallow cloud, as if deciding whether or not to appear. In the distance, a sleek black gelding clomped its hooves against the earth.

Pools of dust stirred, swirling and quickly disappearing.

Lambs frolicked across the parcel of pasture separating the Sommer home from Old Sam Beachy's bright red barn. From where they stood, Rebecca could barely glimpse the orange YIELD sign on the back of the empty buggy parked next to the house.

"I'm the only person Dad trusts with his business." William paused and lowered his voice. "Beth wants me to come to Indiana and run his cabinet shop, Rebecca."

The news caused a wave of anxiety to roll through Rebecca's chest. She wrung her hands together in a nervous gesture. A long silence ensued as she thought of William leaving, and her shoulders grew tense. Not even the light, sweet fragrance floating from her mother's rose garden could take away Rebecca's anxiety.

When she finally started to respond, William held up a defensive hand. "It's just until he's back on his feet. This may not be such a bad thing. The experience might actually benefit us."

Rebecca raised a curious brow. The breeze blew a chestnut-brown hair out of place, and she quickly tucked it back under her *kapp*. Her gaze drifted from his face to his rolled-up sleeves.

Tiny freckles decorated his nose, giving him a youthful appearance. But there was nothing boyish about his square jaw or broad shoulders that tried to push their way out of his shirt. Her heart skipped a beat. She lifted her chin, and their eyes locked in understanding.

William smiled a little. "One of these days, we'll run our own company." He winked. "Don't worry."

She swallowed the lump in her throat. For one blissful, hopeful moment, she trusted everything would be okay. It wasn't those simple two words that reassured her, but the tender, persuasive way William said them. The low, steady tone in which he spoke could convince Rebecca of almost anything.

The warm pink glow on his cheeks made Rebecca's pulse pick up speed. As he looked at her for a reaction, her lips lifted into a wide smile. At the same time, it was impossible to stop the nervous rising and falling of her chest.

She'd never dreamed of being without William. Even temporarily. At the young age of eighteen, she hadn't confronted such a difficult issue.

But her church teachers and parents had raised her to deal with obstacles. Fortunately, they had prepared her to be strong and to pray for guidance. As she stared at her beloved flower garden, her thoughts became more chaotic.

The clothes on the line rose and fell with the warm summer breeze. Their fresh, soapy scent floated through the air. She surely had greater control over her destiny than the wet garments, whose fate was dependent on the wind. She and William could get through this. They loved each other. God would take care of them, wouldn't He?

She glanced up at William. The way the sun hit him at an angle made him look even taller than his six feet and two inches. He'd always been bigger and stronger than other kids his age.

The gray flecks in his deep blue eyes danced to a mysterious tune as he darted her a grin. When she looked into those dark pools, she could drown in happiness. But today, even the warmth emanating from his smile couldn't stop the concern that edged her voice. "Don't worry? But I do, William. What about . . ."

"Us?"

She nodded.

He leveled his gaze so that she looked directly at him. "Nothing has changed. We'll still get married in November after the harvest."

Rebecca hesitated. She couldn't believe William would really leave Arthur, Illinois. But his reason was legitimate. His father needed him. She wasn't selfish, and asking him to stay would be.

Circumstances were beyond her control. What could she do? The question nagged at her until frustration set in. Within a matter of minutes, her world had changed, and she fought to adjust. She nervously tapped the toe of her black shoe against the ground.

As she crossed her arms over her chest, she wished they could protect her from the dilemma she faced. Her brows narrowed into a frown, and a long silence ensued. She looked at him, hoping for an answer. Seeking even a hint of a solution.

To her surprise, William teased, "Rebecca, stop studying me like I'm a map of the world."

His statement broke the tension, and she burst into laughter because a map of the world was such a far stretch from what she'd been thinking.

"Of course, you've got to help your folks, William. I know how much Daniel's business means to him. You certainly can't let him lose it. I can imagine the number of cabinets on order."

Surprised and relieved that her voice sounded steady, Rebecca's shoulders trembled as the thought of William leaving sank in. They'd grown up together and hadn't spent a day without seeing one another.

She stopped a moment and considered Daniel and

Beth Conrad. Nearly a decade ago, William's mamma had died, and Daniel had married Beth.

He was a skilled cabinetmaker. It was no surprise that people from all over the United States ordered his custom-made pieces. Rebecca had seen samples of his elegant, beautiful woodworking.

A thought popped into Rebecca's mind, and she frowned. "William, you seem to be forgetting something very important. Daniel and Beth . . . They're English."

He nodded. "Don't think I haven't given that consideration."

"I don't want to sound pessimistic, but how will you stay Amish in their world?"

He shrugged. "They're the same as us, really."

She rolled her eyes. "Of course they are. But the difference between our lifestyle and theirs is night and day. How can you expect to move in with them and be compatible?"

William hooked his fingers over his trouser pockets, looked down at the ground and furrowed a brow. Rebecca smiled. She knew him so well. Whenever something bothered him, he did this. Rebecca loved the intense look on his face when he worried. The small indentation in his chin intensified.

What fascinated her most, though, were the mysterious gray flecks that danced in his eyes. When he lifted his chin, those flecks took on a metallic appearance. Mesmerized, Rebecca couldn't stop looking at them.

Moments later, as if having made an important decision, he stood still, moved his hands to his hips, and met her gaze with a nod.

In a more confident tone, he spoke. "It will be okay, Rebecca. Don't forget that Dad was Amish before he married Beth. He was raised with the same principles as us. Just because he's English now doesn't mean he's forgotten everything he learned. No need to worry. He won't want me to change."

"No?"

William gave a firm shake of his head. "Of course not. In fact, I'm sure he'll insist that I stick to how I was brought up. Remember, he left me with Aenti Sarah and Uncle John when he remarried. Dad told me that raising me Amish was what my mother would have expected. The *Ordnung* was important to her. And keeping the faith must have also been at the top of Dad's list to have left me here. Nothing will change, Rebecca."

Rebecca realized that she was making too much out of William's going away. After all, it was only Indiana. Not the North Pole! Suddenly embarrassed at her lack of strength, she looked down at the hem of her dress before gazing straight into his eyes. He moved so close, his warm breath caressed her bottom lip, and it quivered. Time seemed to stand still while she savored the silent mutual understanding between them. That unique, unexplainable connection that she and William had.

"I've always read that things happen for a reason," William mentioned.

"Me too." Rebecca also knew the importance of the *Ordnung*. And she knew William's mamma, Miriam, would have wanted him to stay in the faith that had meant everything to her.

As if sensing her distress, he interlaced his fingers together in front of him. His hands were large. She'd watched those very hands lift heavy bales of hay.

"Who knows? Maybe this is God's way of testing me."

Rebecca gave an uncertain roll of her eyes. "Talk to your aunt and uncle. They'll know what's best. After all, they've raised you since your father remarried."

The frustration in William's voice lifted a notch. "I already did. It's hard to convince them that what I'm doing is right." He lowered his voice. "You know how they feel. When Dad left the faith, he deserted me. But even so, I can't turn my back on him."

"Of course not."

"Aenti Sarah's concerned that people will treat me differently when I come back. She wants to talk to the bishop and get his permission. If that makes her feel better, then I'm all for it."

"If he'll give his blessing."

William nodded in agreement.

"But we're old enough to think for ourselves, William. When we get married and raise our family, we can't let everyone make up our minds for us."

He raised a brow. "You're so independent, Miss Rebecca."

She smiled a little.

A mischievous twinkle lightened his eyes.

"Your decision shouldn't be based on what people think," Rebecca said. "If we made choices to please others, we'd never win. Deep down inside, we have to be happy with ourselves. So you've got to do what's in your heart. And no one can decide that but you."

The expression that crossed his face suddenly became unreadable. She tilted her head and studied him with immense curiosity. "What are you thinking?"

His gray flecks repeated that metallic appearance. "Rebecca, you're something else."

A surge of warmth rushed through her.

"I can't believe your insight." He blinked in amazement. "You're an angel." His voice was low and soft. She thought he was going to kiss her. But he didn't. William followed the church rules. But Rebecca wouldn't have minded breaking that one.

In a breathless voice, she responded, "Thank you for that."

As if suddenly remembering the crux of their conversation, William returned to the original topic. "I've assured Aenti Sarah and Uncle John that I won't leave the Amish community. That I'll come back, and we'll get married. They finally justified letting me leave by looking at this as an opportunity to explore *Rumspringa*."

Rebecca grinned. "I guess that's one way to look at it." Rumspringa was the transition time between adolescence and adulthood when an Amish youth could try things before deciding whether to join the faith for him—or herself. She even had a friend who had gone as far as to get a driver's license.

He paused. "Rebecca, I know we didn't plan on this." His voice grew more confident as he continued. "You've got to understand that I love you more than anything in the world. Please tell me you'll wait for me. I give you my word that this move is only temporary. As soon as Dad's on his feet again, I'll come home. Promise."

As William committed, Rebecca took in his dark brown hair. The sun's brightness lightened it to the color of sand. For a moment, his features were both rugged and endearing. Rebecca's heart melted.

Her voice softened. "How long do you think you'll stay?"

William pressed his lips together thoughtfully. "Good

question. Hopefully, he'll be back to work in no time. His customers depend on him, and according to Beth, he has a long list of orders for cabinets to produce and deliver. He's a strong man, Rebecca. He'll be okay."

"I believe that. I'll never forget when he came into town last year to see you." She giggled. "Remember his fancy car?"

William chuckled. "He sure enjoys the luxuries of the English. I wish our community wouldn't be so harsh on him. He's really Amish at heart."

William hesitated. "I used to resent that he left me."

Long moments passed in silence. He stepped closer and lowered his voice to a whisper. "Rebecca, you've become unusually quiet. And you didn't answer my question."

She raised an inquisitive brow.

"Will you wait for me?"

Her thoughts were chaotic. For something to do, she looked down and flattened her hands against her long, brown dress. She realized how brave William was and recalled the scandal Daniel Conrad had made when he married outside of the faith and had moved to the country outside of Evansville, Indiana. She raised her chin to look at William's face. Mamma always told her that a person's eyes gave away his feelings.

The tongue could lie. But not the eyes. William's intriguing flecks had become a shade lighter, dancing with hope and sincerity. His cheeks were flushed.

"William, you've got to do this." She let out a small, thoughtful sigh. "I remember a particular church sermon from a long time ago. The message was that our success in life isn't determined by making easy choices. It's measured by how we deal with difficult issues. And leaving Arthur is definitely a tough decision."

He hugged his hands to his hips. "What are you getting at?"

She quietly sought an answer to his question. What did she mean? She'd sounded like she knew what she was talking about. Moments later, the answer came. She recognized it with complete clarity.

She squared her shoulders. "I promised you I'd stick by you forever, William. And right now, you need me."

He gazed down at her in confusion.

Clearing her throat, she looked up at him and drew a long breath. "I'm going with you."

Inside Old Sam Beachy's barn, Rebecca poured out her dilemma to her dear friend. Afterwards, Buddy whimpered sympathetically at her feet. Rebecca reached down from her rocking chair opposite Old Sam's workbench and obediently stroked the Irish setter behind his ears. The canine closed his eyes in contentment.

Old Sam was famous for his hope chests. He certainly wasn't the only person to put together the pieces, but he was a brilliant artist who etched beautiful, personalized designs into the lids.

Rebecca had looked at his beloved Esther as a second mother. Since she'd succumbed to pneumonia a couple of years ago, Rebecca had tried to return her kindness to the old widower. So did her friends, Rachel and Annie. The trio took care of him. Rachel listened to Sam's horse-and-buggy stories. Annie baked him delicious sponge cakes while Rebecca picked him fresh flowers.

Drawing a long breath, Rebecca wondered what advice he'd give. Whatever it was would be good. Because no one was wiser than Old Sam. She crossed her legs at the ankles. Sawdust floated in the air. Rebecca breathed in the woodsy smell of oak.

When he started to speak, she sat up a little straighter. "The real secret to happiness is not what we give or receive; it's what we share. I would consider your help to William and his parents a gift from the heart. At the same time, a clear conscience is a soft pillow. You want to have the blessing of our bishop and your parents. The last thing you want is a scandal about you and William living under the same roof."

Rebecca let out a deep, thoughtful sigh as she considered his wisdom. In the background, she could hear Ginger enter her stall from the pasture. Old Sam's horse snorted. And that meant she wanted an apple.

Sam's voice prompted Rebecca to meet his gaze. "Rebecca, I can give you plenty of advice. But the most important thing I can tell you is to pray."

Rebecca nodded and crossed her arms over her chest.

"But remember: Do not ask the Lord to guide your footsteps if you're not willing to move your feet."

Rebecca was fully aware that William was ready to leave. In her front yard, she hugged her baby sister, Emily, shoving a rebellious strand of blond hair out of her face. Rebecca planted an affectionate kiss on brother Peter's cheek. "Be good."

Pete's attention was on Rebecca just long enough to say good-bye. As she turned to her father, the two kids started screaming and chasing each other in a game of tag. Emily nearly tripped over a chicken in the process. Rebecca was quick to notice the uncertain expression on Old Sam's face.

The sweet, creamy smell of homemade butter competed with the aroma of freshly baked bread. Both enticing scents floated out of the open kitchen windows. Tonight, Rebecca would miss Mamma's dinner. It would be the first time Rebecca hadn't eaten with her family.

Her heart pumped to an uncertain beat. But she'd never let her fear show. Ever since the death of her other little sister, Rebecca had learned to put on a brave façade. Her family depended on her for strength.

Rebecca's father grasped her hands and gave them a tight squeeze. She immediately noted that his arms shook. It stunned her to realize that his embrace was more of a nervous gesture than an offer of support. And the expression on his face was anything but encouraging. Rebecca understood his opposition to what she was about to do. Her father's approval was important to her, and it bothered her to seem disrespectful.

All of her life, she'd tried hard to please him. They'd never even argued. In fact, this was the first time she'd gone against his wishes. But William was her future. She wanted to be by his side whenever he needed her.

In a gruff, firm voice, her father spoke. "Be careful, Becca. You know how I feel. I'm disappointed that William hasn't convinced you to stay. You belong here. In Arthur."

He pushed out a frustrated breath. "But you're of age to make your own decision. We've made arrangements with Beth so that living under the same roof with William will be proper. We trust she'll be a responsible chaperone while you're with the Conrads. Just come home soon. We need your help with chores."

He pointed an authoritative finger. "And never let the English ways influence you. They will tempt you to be like them, Becca. Remember your faith."

Rebecca responded with a teary nod. When she finally faced Mamma, she forced a brave smile. But the tightness in her throat made it difficult to say good-bye.

Mamma's deep blue eyes clouded with moisture. With one swift motion, Rebecca hugged her. For long moments, she was all too aware of how much she would miss that security. The protection only a parent could offer.

Much too soon, Mamma released her and held her at arm's length. When Rebecca finally turned to Old Sam, he stepped forward and handed her a cardboard container with handles.

She met his gaze and lifted a curious brow. "This is for me?"

He nodded. "I hope you like it." He pointed. "Go ahead. Take it out."

Everyone was quiet while she removed the gift. As she lifted the hope chest, she caught her breath. There was a unanimous sound of awe from the group. "Old Sam . . ." She focused on the design etched into the lid. "It's absolutely beautiful! I will treasure it the rest of my life."

"You always bring me fresh flowers, so I thought you'd like the bouquet."

She glanced at William before turning her attention back to Sam. "I'm taking the miniature hope chest with me."

Sam's voice was low and edged with emotion. "I will pray for your safety. And remember that freedom is not to do as you please, but the liberty to do as you ought.

And the person who sows seeds of kindness will have a perpetual harvest. That's you, Rebecca."

Rebecca blinked as salty tears filled her eyes. With great care, she returned the hope chest to its box on the bright green blades of grass.

Old Sam's voice cracked. "You come back soon. And if you want good advice, consult an old man." A grin tugged at Rebecca's lips. Sam knew every proverb in the book. She'd miss hearing him recount them.

"Thank you again. I can't wait to start putting away special trinkets for the children I will have some day."

When she looked up at him, he merely nodded approval.

William's voice startled her from her thoughts. "Rebecca, it's time to head out. It's gonna be a long drive."

Her gaze remained locked with Mamma's. Mary Sommer's soft voice shook with emotion. "This is the first time you've left us. But you're strong."

Rebecca squeezed her eyes closed for several heartbeats.

As if to reassure herself, her mother went on. "We hope Daniel recovers quickly. William needs you. In the meantime, God will keep both of you in His hands. Don't forget that. Always pray. And remember what we've taught you. Everything you've learned in church."

"*Jah.*"

"It's never been a secret that God gave you a special gift for accepting challenges. I'll never forget the time you jumped into that creek to save your brother. You pulled him to shore."

Rebecca grinned. "I remember."

"Rumspringa might be the most important time in your life. But be very careful. There will be temptations in the English world. In fact, the bishop is concerned that you will decide against joining the Amish church."

"I know who I am."

A tear rolled down Mamma's cheek while she slipped something small and soft between Rebecca's palms. Rebecca glanced down at the crocheted cover.

"I put together this Scripture book to help you while you're away, Rebecca. When you have doubts or fears, read it. The good words will comfort and give you strength. You can even share them with Beth. She's going through a difficult time. Your *daed* and I will pray for you every day." She paused. "Lend Daniel your support. The bishop wants you to set three additional goals and accomplish them while you're gone. Give them careful consideration. They must be unselfish and important. Doing this will make your mission even more significant."

After a lengthy silence, William addressed the Sommers in a reassuring voice. "I'll take good care of her. You can be sure of that."

Rebecca's dad raised his chin and directed his attention to William. "We expect nothing less."

Long, tense moments passed while her father and William locked gazes. Several heartbeats later, Eli Sommer stepped forward. "I don't approve of my Becca going so far away. I'm holding you responsible for her, William. If anything happens . . ."

William darted an unsure glance at Rebecca before responding. "I understand your concern. That's why I didn't encourage her to come."

Rebecca raised her chin and regarded both of them. "I've given this a lot of thought. I'll go. And I'll come back, safe and sound."

Rebecca listened with dread as her father continued making his case. She knew William wouldn't talk back. And she wasn't about to change her mind about going.

"Daed, it's my decision. Please don't worry."

Before he could argue, she threw her arms around him and gave him a tight, reassuring hug. After she stepped away, William motioned toward the black Cadillac. As Rebecca drew a deep breath, her knees trembled, and her heart pounded like a jackhammer. Finally, she forced her jellylike legs to move. She didn't turn around as William opened her door.

Before stepping inside, Rebecca put Mamma's scripture book inside the hope chest. William took the box from her and placed it in the middle of the backseat. Rebecca brought very little with her. Just one small suitcase that her father placed in the trunk.

With great hesitation, she waved good-bye. She forced a confident smile, but her entire body shook. She sat very still as Daniel's second cousin, Ethan, backed the car out of the drive. Gravel crunched under the tires. This wasn't Rebecca's first ride in an automobile. Car rides were not uncommon in the Amish community.

Trying to convince herself she was doing the right thing, she gently pushed the down arrow by her door handle, and the window opened. Rebecca turned in her seat and waved until the sad faces of her family, their plain-looking wooden-framed house built by her great-grandfather, and Old Sam, disappeared.

William turned to her. A worry crease crept across his forehead. The cleft in his chin became more pronounced. "Rebecca, your dad's right. I should have made you

stay. The last thing I want to do is create tension between you two."

"It wasn't your choice. As far as my father's concerned . . ." She gave a frustrated shake of her head. "I don't like displeasing him either. On the other hand, it's not right for me to stay here and send you off to save Daniel's shop all by yourself." She shrugged.

In silence, she thought about what she'd just said. She nervously ran her hand over the smooth black leather seat.

"You can adjust the air vents," Ethan announced, turning briefly to make eye contact with her.

She was thankful she didn't have to travel to the Indiana countryside by horse and buggy. She rather enjoyed the soft, barely audible purring of the engine.

Next to her, she eyed the cardboard and pulled out the mini hope chest, setting the box on the floor. She smiled a little.

"Old Sam is something else." William's voice was barely more than a whisper.

"*Jah.* I can't wait to tell him about our trip." Rebecca giggled. "I'll miss listening to him grumble while he works in the barn. I enjoy watching him make those elaborate chests that he sells to the stores in town."

William gave a small nod. "He loves you three girls."

"Thank goodness that Annie and Rachel will be around to keep him company."

The three friends had loved Esther. Now they took care of Old Sam. He was like an uncle to them. But Rebecca was leaving the world she knew. Would she fit in with the English?